Violators

By Fran Hinton

© 2/10/13

Preface

Just a small note from the author ... nothing droll or boring that might take up too much time. Time is such a valuable commodity, second only to our children, the other valuable that we share worldwide.

I would like to say before going any further that this novel is not meant to be taken as any form of symbolism. I merely felt the need to express my opinions on where this country continues to go with it's youth. Here are a few factors for every one of us to consider, even if you set this book down, never intending to turn another page.

If there were fewer homeless children in the United States of America, maybe we wouldn't have quite so hard a time keeping track of them.

When there continue to be so many issues with runaway children why aren't we doing something about the reasons that they are running away?

Why are there so many problems with our school systems that they consistently make the evening news? Shouldn't we have rolled with the changes in efforts to properly respond to the national problems with children? The children that we expect to keep things going after we are long gone?

Yes. I know that I make it all sound too simple. I realize that it's not. That is what baffles me. My point is that it should be.

We have the knowledge and will power to launch an aircraft into outer space, end the Cold War, and tear down the Berlin Wall. Yet when it comes to our most valuable commodity, our children, we seem to not have the time, the resources to spare in dedication to our young future.

I will dedicate this novel to my brothers and sisters. I hope that they, wherever they may be at the time have the opportunity to read these pages. I hope that they will understand why I did the things that I did, said the things that were said, lived the way that I lived. I hope in time, that they will forgive me.

Please remember, throughout this novel, that it is fiction based on fact. The Violators are real. They are out there. Consider the possibilities and the realities of the positions that we have put our children in. I hate thinking that maybe, just maybe, I have been allowed a glimpse of the future that I, as a parent, dread.

Best Intentions, Fran Hinton

Chapter One

Michelle stepped out of her apartment into the small corridor that led to the street. She wrapped her scarf tightly around her neck to keep off the brunt of the cold wind that howled outside. She grimaced. One of these days, she would buy a car.

She inched her way across the street to the entrance of the park. It was a shorter distance this way to where she worked. Whatever it took to save on walking distance this morning. The wind blowing off of the lake was freezing cold.

As she worked her way through the park she ran over a mental checklist of things she needed to accomplish in the next few months. It wasn't much, a car, a decent place to live, a savings account and to move far, far away from her father.

It seemed, no matter how hard that she tried, that they just could not get along. Neither of them was very good at forgetting the past. Neither of them had been very good at forgiving, either.

Michelle stopped suddenly, noticing what appeared to be blond hair behind a tree to her right. How odd, with this weather, for someone to be lounging beneath a tree.

She shrugged it off and continued on her way. There were stranger things known to happen in this town. Chicago had a great many freaky occurrences. Every great city did.

No matter how hard she tried she could not ignore the feeling that something was very wrong. Before she made it another thirty feet, she turned back.

Sure enough, when she arrived back at the same spot, the blond hair appeared to be in the exact same position. There had to be something wrong. No one could not move in this freezing cold.

Michelle drew nearer the tree, taking in the sight of very white feet and legs. Michelle hesitated, not going any further for fear of what she might see. Yet, in the same instant, she had to go on. What if the person were badly hurt? Or worse?

Michelle grimaced and took another step closer to the base of the tree. There, lying completely nude was the body of a young girl.

She shrank back in terror, grabbing the trunk of the tree for support. After taking a few deep breaths and calming herself, she forced herself to touch the cheek of the girl. The body was ice cold.

Michelle leaned down for a closer inspection. There were no obvious signs of violence that she could see. The girl seemed to be frozen solid.

She stood straight and shook her head hard. She had to think clearly of what she should do next. She took off her coat, intending to cover the girl, then put it back on, deciding that it would do the poor child no good now. She would need it for the walk back towards the apartment and the pay phone.

She set off at a determined pace, not wanting to think of the dead girl lying on the ground. Michelle didn't even want to start trying to figure out the how and why of it all. That was not important right now. Right now she needed some cops.

Michelle made it to the phone and dialed 911.

A female voice inquired to whether or not it was an emergency.

She answered that it was.

The operator told her to hold the line and someone would be right with her.

Michelle held patiently for about five minutes and was toying with the notion of trying again when the operator picked back up.

She bit her lip periodically, fighting to remain calm while explaining that she'd been on her way to work and discovered the body of a dead girl.

The operator told her to stay where she was; a squad was in the area and would be right with her. She was asked to please hold the line until the officers in the area arrived.

Michelle blocked her out. There were other thoughts running crazily through her head, non-stop.

She didn't know how long she stood there with the operator going on and on when she spotted the cop car out of the corner of her eye. She didn't even think to tell the operator that they had arrived; she just hung up the phone.

A blond California surfer type stepped out of the car towards Michelle asking if she were the one to call in the report.

Michelle looked around and replied that no one else would be stupid enough to stand out here in the cold.

He laughed, throwing his head back, before giving her an easy smile. He turned, without saying another word and went back to the police car. He gave a nod to his partner confirming that she made the call. He popped the trunk and grabbed a thick coat and blanket before returning to offer them to her.

She gratefully took the blanket and wrapped it tightly around her while he bundled himself into the coat.

"Michelle Warren, is that correct miss?"

Michelle nodded her head that it was.

"We really appreciate your call. I know that it is very cold out here today but I'd really be grateful if you could lead us back to that body."

Michelle only nodded her head again. She'd better say something soon or they would think that she were in shock or something. She almost laughed out loud as the thought crossed her mind that they would have to admit her to a sanitarium now. Laughing at a dead body in front of the cops. They were probably thinking that she had totally lost it.

The surfer cop and his partner merely exchanged glances. He then gestured for her to lead the way.

Michelle quieted her thoughts and began concentrating on retracing her steps. When they came to the spot where they could see the blond hair, she pointed.

The officers both went over to the tree. They had only been gone a few moments when the surfer cop came back, taking her by the elbow and steering her in the direction of the parked squad. "Mind if we go and sit in the squad car where it's warm?"

"Sure." Michelle answered. They had only gone a few steps when Michelle came to an abrupt halt. She took the blanket off of her shoulders and looked up at him imploringly. "Please go back and cover her up. I know that sounds dumb, but I would really feel a lot better if you would."

The surfer cop nodded and taking the blanket, went back over behind the tree.

Once he returned they headed for the car.

When they had gotten in, she waited while the cop called in to verify the body. He switched on the heater full blast and lit a cigarette.

He looked over at her, gesturing at the smoke that was curling around his face. "Do you mind?"

Michelle shook her head. "No, as a matter of fact, I could use one of those myself."

The surfer cop obligingly shook another cigarette out of the pack and lit it before handing it to her. "I've been trying to quit but every time that I see something like that, whoosh, my resolve flies right out the window."

Michelle nodded her head in agreement. "Yes, I can see how that would happen. I know that when I first saw her the only thing going through my head was to run."

He stubbed out his cigarette and turned to face her. "I really hate to ask, especially when I am pretty sure I can guess how you found her, but I have to be sure."

"Of course." Michelle nodded and took a long drag before going back through every detail of what she had seen and done that morning. She even included the impulse to reach down and touch the dead girl's cheek.

The surfer cop nodded periodically, showing his thoughts with a frown here and there.

When she finished, he asked a few questions, verifying what she had told him.

"Well, Michelle," he said finally, "there will

probably be a whole lot of cops all wanting to ask you the same shit that I just did. Be strong. Try and keep your cool. And try not to smoke more than a pack a day."

He patted her shoulder with a small smile and got out of the car to talk to other officers that had begun to arrive.

Michelle allowed herself a smile as she watched two detectives approach her surfer cop. She looked down as he gestured to her. She was sure that he was right. Not only about being questioned for the next forty-eight hours straight but about trying not to smoke more than a pack a day.

CHAPTER TWO

Steven hurried, trying desperately to keep up with Wes. What was the big hurry for now anyway? They had hauled ass for about thirty minutes non-stop. Surely they could slow down now. His chest was wheezing at an impossible rate.

He glanced around for a second, watching his friends backs disappear around a clump of bushes. He began to run again trying to catch up and tripped over a dead bush, landing face first in the dirty snow.

He struggled to get up and then thought better of it. He would lay here until the thumping in his chest slowed down. He took a few deep breaths and exhaled them slowly, remembering what the doctor had said about his asthma.

Just when he thought he was ready to try and sit up, he heard footsteps off to his right. He looked around slowly, hoping to see some sign of Wes coming back for him.

Not seeing anyone, he headed for the nearest tree that looked sturdy enough to hold him. Thomas always said that you had a better chance on higher ground. If ever at risk, climb a tree.

After getting himself situated in a spot where he could look around without being spotted, he located the source of the footsteps. There was a short skinny lady wearing a purple scarf walking about thirty yards to his right.

He watched quietly as she moved past him never noticing that he was just above her head.

After she had gone another fifty yards, he began looking around in earnest for some sign of Wes coming back for him.

Realizing that his friend was nowhere in sight came as a shock to Steven. He definitely did not want to be alone right now. Not when he was sure that the lady had spotted Carrie's body.

He tried to calm himself and began to make his way down the tree only to stop when he saw the young woman turned around and headed straight for him.

He froze in terror. But the woman just kept heading on in the direction of where Carrie had been left.

As soon as she were well enough out of ear shot he scurried down the tree and hurried in the general direction of where he had last seen Wes. What in the hell was Thomas thinking anyway. The entire scene had gotten way out of hand. It made some of the others wonder if Thomas were thinking clearly.

Everyone knew that he would turn sixteen in three more months. That was why he'd been teaching Josie how to handle the group's movements. Maybe it was for the best that things were headed in that direction.

Steven could imagine how it felt to know that you would only be allowed to live a few more months. His father had threatened him all the time. It wouldn't have been so bad at home if Steven had trusted that his father wouldn't kill him. That was the problem. He knew that he was serious. That was how he wound up here.

He'd joined the group about a year ago. He had gotten sick and tired of the beatings and wondering when his father would finish him off. He was sure that he'd killed his sister. She wouldn't stop crying in the middle of the night and his father had gone in there with a pillow. Steven never saw the baby again. What was to say he wasn't next? His father had beaten him so badly that night that it was nearly three months before he could see out of his left eye again.

Just two months later, his mother committed suicide. Having lost his only protection from his father, he'd packed his things after dad had passed out drunk one night and hit the road.

He'd lived in an abandoned warehouse in Cicero for about two months when he met Josie.

Josie took him back with her to the rest of the group and they convinced him that it would be safer to travel with them than be on his own. After two months spent alone, half starved and having the shit beat out of him regularly, he was sure that she was right.

The part that they didn't tell him was that they never let anyone leave.

Of course, Steven understood all of this now. They were at great risk. They couldn't have anyone just up and leave, taking the chance of being discovered. Thomas called it the greater good. It was a worthy rule.

A movement over to his left brought his attention back to the here and now. It was Wes. He was waving his hand that Steven should stay right where he was for the time being.

That was cool with Steven. He could use the time to rest. His chest still felt like it could burst. Asthma was a bitch of a disease.

He wondered if he would ever out grow it. When Mom had taken him to the doctor a few years before she had died, the doctor had sounded pretty sure that he would. Steven hoped so. It made him feel less useful than the others in the group. He couldn't last as long as most of the other boys.

Oh, no one ever said anything about it, which was cool. But he knew that he wasn't sent to do things as often as some of the others. He was really surprised to be sent with Wes this morning.

Thomas had wakened them at three in the morning to take care of Carrie. She had tried to run.

Steven didn't blame her. It must be really tough to know that you are going to die, especially by a friend's hand.

That was another cardinal rule. No one was allowed to live past the age of sixteen. They were afraid that you would turn out like your parents. If they didn't let you live past the age of sixteen they were sure that you would never have any children to harm.

It sounded cruel in a way. But to them, the children of the group, it made perfect sense.

Wes finally began to signal him to move to him.

Steven cautiously made his way in that direction.

He wondered how Wes felt knowing that he had to die in three years. Steven was only eleven. He had plenty of time to go.

Chapter Three

Josie stared down at the two boys headed in her direction. She hoped that everything had gone all right. It seemed to have taken a lot longer than it should have this time. Of course, the way that it had gone down from the beginning was not the norm.

Josie was used to things going smoothly. She would like to see them stay that way but with Thomas going to God soon, things would never be the same again. It couldn't be avoided. When you turned sixteen, it was your time to go. It was a protective measure that they were sworn to. It had been that way since Josie had joined the group.

She slid gracefully down from her perch in the tree, greeting the boys with a wide grin. "Everything go O.K.?"

Both boys shook their heads no.

Josie stepped between them, threading her arms through their elbows as they walked side by side.

"You guys get the move ready?" Wes

questioned, glancing at the slight girls face out of the corner of his eye.

Josie nodded her head and went on for a moment about how upset Tracy had been over the loss of a tent pole. It was otherwise quiet as they made their way to the new camp. It wasn't far now, another mile or so.

Wes asked if Thomas were prepared for trouble soon.

Josie eyed him questioningly. "Of course he is Wes. We were expecting something to come undone with Carrie. She's always been so high strung."

Steven and Wes traded a long look. The two of them had discussed the fact that the entire group would have to move out of the park as quickly as possible.

It was usually no big deal. It was just an added headache to have to move during the day. They had a couple of youngsters, who did well on the move; it was just more time consuming. It always went quicker when the little ones were moved at night and slept in their sleds.

The trio continued on in silence through the woods. They were used to traveling in the brush and had become adept at doing so with little to no noise. They were no longer talking, each lost in their own thoughts for the moment. They would have time to talk later.

Josie thought again of the rules. It seemed that since she begun to train to take Thomas's spot as leader she was always thinking of the rules.

She wondered just what had gone through Carrie's head before she had died. It seemed so unfair sometimes though they all accepted that it was necessary.

She considered the fact that all had gone well for the group over the last year. They had no trouble finding what they needed to get by for a change. Josie could remember when things had not gone as well for the group.

She had joined the group seven years ago with her brother Patrick.

Beautiful Patrick. He was five years her senior and had gone to join God in peace just over a year ago. The difference had been how happy he was about it. Oh, they did not consider themselves a religious group. Several of the other kids used language that would make the Pope blush. They were just sure that when they went to God, they would be committing far less sins than the adults who had raised them.

Patrick, for example, was burned severely when their mother had found him in the cookie jar, and forced both hands over the stove top's open flames. That was why she was with the group. Patrick decided that she would be safe if gotten away from their parents.

Their parents were both crack addicts. There had been another sister who died at birth.

Patrick had just turned nine and she five when he packed her up and headed for the hills. He hid bags behind the garage the night before and when they left for school in the morning, they simply kept on going.

She wondered sometimes what her mother and father were doing now. She didn't really care, she was just curious.

When Patrick had gone to God she had been glad, almost envious. How wonderful to spend eternity in peace with your Maker.

It was odd that now she pondered the reality of the answers to it all.

Well she would never know, would she? She had turned thirteen six months ago and would go gladly when the time came, as her brother had before her. She would not cause the group all of the trouble that Carrie had.

They finally arrived at the make shift camp where the others were in a large circle, eating a cold breakfast.

Thomas rose and came to meet them when he saw the trio approach. "How did it go?"

Wes shook his head negatively. "Not good at all. We really need to haul ass out of here."

Thomas nodded and walked back to stand in the center of the circle. "We have to move to another park, quickly and quietly."

Thomas walked back to the trio. "Well, what happened?"

"I saw a lady." Steven informed him, looking over to Wes for support. "I don't know if she saw Carrie or not, but I have the feeling that she did."

Thomas looked curiously from one to the other.

Wes shrugged his shoulders.

Thomas beckoned to the rest of the group, shaking his head. "Well, we don't have time to discuss it now. It will have to wait until we make the train."

The group assembled around the three, Shelley grabbing Steven's hand and Emily finding Josie's arm.

Josie smiled and picked up the pretty little three year old, folding her safely into her arms.

Thomas gave a low whistle and the group headed north through the wooded area of the park.

Chapter Four

Thomas listened carefully as Wes and Steven filled him in on how and where they had placed Carrie. They explained how they had gotten split up and how they had both seen the lady at different times in different places.

Thomas only nodded his head and traded glances with Josie from time to time. He wondered what she thought about the entire situation. He watched as she narrowed her eyes and let a light frown drift across her features. He wondered if she had a plan on how to handle all of this.

Wes finished the talk with how he had seen the lady start in one direction and then turn and head back towards where they had left Carrie. He concluded that he thought it would be very safe to assume that she had been found.

Thomas flinched physically. His original plan did not include moving as quickly as this would call for. The group was not prepared.

Josie questioned Wes about how long the lady had stayed near the area where Carrie's body lie.

Wes shrugged and replied that he thought about five minutes.

She asked how the woman looked when she'd walked away.

Wes just shook his head.

Steven said that he was not close enough to see her face, though she seemed like she was hurrying.

Josie and Thomas looked at each other, prompting Thomas to get up and pace. "The two of you should get some rest while Josie and I decide how to work this out."

The two boys hastily left the fallen tree that had been their seats during the interview and went in search of a couple of blankets to curl up in.

Josie stood and put an arm around the pacing Thomas. "Don't worry. We'll manage. We always do."

Thomas shook his head negatively. "We haven't got enough food built up to hop a train yet Josie. The children have not had enough rest from the last move."

Josie nodded in understanding. "It's going to be tricky. We'll have to send Tracy and John into the city while the rest of us head for the tracks and the jump. True, there won't be much time for rest but everyone sleeps well on the train. Well, except you."

Thomas nodded his head in agreement. Josie was definitely catching on to how things needed to be done. She did especially well in stressful situations, which were his downfall.

He walked silently to the center of the clearing that served as an impromptu camp. He waved his hands, beckoning for the rest of his family to draw near.

He studied Steven carefully wondering how his asthma would hold up in the rush. Last thing they needed was a severe attack right now. He would do what he could to keep Steven's workload to a minimum.

"Tracy, John, I need the two of you to go with Josie for instructions and a tough supply list. I wish you the best of luck. The rest of us will have to rely on what you can scrounge up for the next couple of days."

The blond, blue-eyed pair went off to find Josie in the only tent that they would have to take down.

Thomas smiled as he watched the pair go.

They were so alike to leek at; it was a wonder that they weren't brother and sister. Of his entire group that he could send, these two were the most efficient in getting what they would need.

He beckoned to Wes, who had been roused from his blanket only to look more exhausted. "I know that you've not had any rest but it will have to wait. We simply cannot risk the possibility that woman spotted Carrie. We have to hop a train."

He spoke to Wes, but others gathered around to listen in. "I want you to prepare the youngsters. We're going to be traveling in the daylight, so we have to move separately." Thomas paused and looked over the crowd of faces that had gathered. He smiled slightly and took a deep breath before continuing.

"Wes, after you get the little ones ready, you are to take charge of Emily and Kevin. Nancy, you will assist Wes and be in charge of Darryl and Lil' Dawn. Shelley, you may go with Steven and Josie. I will give instructions on where we will join up as soon as the people in charge are through with the moving preparations. Let me know when you are ready.

He studied the group of young faces all

turned towards him. "Don't worry. I know that this is sudden and it's going to be different from the way that we usually travel but we will manage just fine."

He smiled at his family and turned back towards the only tent. He would have to secure his maps and papers before they could take it down. He would have to decide the best place for them to rejoin, with luck, before midday.

After gathering everything into his case he went to study his map beneath a tree.

He was thinking that it would be in their best interest to take a train out as soon as they could get one - anywhere. It would be in the best interest of their continued safety and guarantee them the rest they needed.

Josie approached silently, watching him study train schedules and maps alternately until he looked up. "Things are going great. We are ready to rock and roll in ten."

Thomas gave her a weak smile. "Great. It will be a relief to get clear of here." He studied his friend and main confidant closely for a moment. "Sit here with me and see what you think."

Josie settled down next to him and together

they studied the map. She took the railroad schedules and pointed to the park that they had intended to move to before the chaos with Carrie began. "We're only a half mile off of the main here, Thomas." She pointed. Surely they will have some freight cars within the next couple of miles that they intend to pick up tonight. Can we wait it out till dark and hop then?"

Thomas studied her proposed route for a moment. "We'll meet at the park and scout it out beforehand." He shook his head. "The babies will be exhausted."

Josie nodded her head. "It's a necessary evil in this case. We should get out of town and fast. According to this the next hop is in East Peoria. That's a good spot. It's less than a mile from the camp to the park to set up camp. Plenty of thick cover, once we get situated. And there's plenty of shopping and we can stock up and rest before we head further south."

"Excellent. It will be a tough run but I think, depending on how John and Tracy do in town, that we can manage."

Josie smiled reassuringly. "We'll ration the food if need be. Knowing those two though, knowing the situation like they do, I have a feeling we will be just fine."

She went on to explain where she was to meet them with the first load of supplies and copied directions for the both of them to the spot where they were to rejoin.

Thomas got to his feet. "Cross your fingers." He pulled her to her feet next to him. The first of the leaders were headed towards him.

Josie watched as he gave directions on where they would rejoin. He handled things calmly and with the entire groups best interest in mind. Would she always manage to do the same?

Chapter Five

The moving of the children was one of the most difficult tasks that the group faced. They would have to move in small groups of twos and threes. They would need to go through town as quickly as they could manage not drawing unwanted attentions.

In the four years that Thomas had led the group, they had always been successful. He always picked the twos and threes according to who looked alike. The older children led the younger and they passed off as brother and sister.

The hard part was the little ones. Emily had just turned three. He sent her with Wes this time because Wes was third in command. They looked somewhat alike and he could count on Wes to move non-stop until they reached the rejoin spot.

Each group would leave at ten-minute intervals, Wes going first with the youngest, Emily. Wes could be counted on to find a secluded spot and readying things for the arrival of the others.

It would be much the same with the other groups. It would take them awhile this way. If Carrie's body had indeed already been discovered it had to be done this way.

They had to get everyone back together and secure by nightfall. There was no practical way to travel through town with a baby and not look suspicious if you are only thirteen.

Thomas nodded to Wes, the first to leave with Kevin and Emily. "I need for you three to get started." He indicated the area marked in red on the map. "Here's where you need to end up. You can take the short route, going right through town or you can take the long way, near these warehouses. I figured I'd leave that part up to you."

Wes shook his head. "What would you do Tom? Do you think it's safe for me to have Emily in town during the day?"

Thomas studied his friend's face for a moment. "Yes, I think since it's only mid-morning that you could cross through these areas with no problem."

"That's the way we'll go then. How long do you think it will take us to make the tracks?"

"About two and a half hours, maybe three

with both Kevin and Emily." Thomas shrugged his shoulders. "It would be good if you can make it there with enough time to find a clearing between the park and the tracks for us to sit awhile."

Wes grinned. "I'll do my best."

"I know that you will." Thomas patted his shoulder. "That's part of why you go first."

Josie came up behind Wes. "Looks like every thing's packed up tight. Are you ready to go? I just took Emily to the bathroom, so she should be good to go for at least an hour. Longer if you are lucky."

The threesome laughed. Emily was a typical three-year old. She had been hell to potty train. After it had been accomplished, it had become her favorite game.

"I'm not all that worried. I think I can persuade her to wait, unless it's an emergency..." Wes chuckled. "I have a way with her."

Josie smiled her agreement. "Emily definitely has a crush on you Wes. It's good that you can use that to your advantage."

Thomas looked around at the others who had

gathered around them. "Are we ready to get started?"

The group nodded agreement.

"Let's set the first off then."

The entire group moved as one through the park in silence to where the tree line thinned to make way for a deep clearing. The sidewalk for a nature trail ran about forty feet from where the group would sit and wait their turns to leave. The waiting in this case seemed as difficult as the traveling. They would have to be silent. They would be worrying how the others were managing as they crossed the town.

Hugs and kisses were exchanged with each of the family with Josie and Thomas the last.

Josie hugged Wes tightly to her and kissed Emily on the cheek, whispering in her ear.

Thomas smiled to himself. Wes was not the only one who had a way with the feisty three year old.

Thomas firmly grasped Wes by the hand before hugging him close. "Time to go."

Josie looked at her watch and nodded. She would keep track of the exact starts to record later.

Wes gathered Emily in his arms, settling her carefully on his hip. He grabbed Kevin's hand and set off at a quick pace.

Thomas allowed himself a smile. He was sure that Wes would have no problems. Even with the terrible twosome.

Thomas walked back into the clearing to the woods and crouched at the feet of Nancy, who had Lil' Dawn and Darryl already in her lap. He showed her the map. He would not leave the route up to Nancy as he had with Wes.

He would send these three the long way. Nancy was less experienced and had the two rowdiest children in the group.

It would give Wes a few extra minutes to get situated. He would follow the short route with Shelley and Josie would head deep into the city to meet Tracy and John with supplies.

After he explained to Nancy in hushed tones what he wanted her to do and where she would stop, he headed back to Josie and Shelley. He sat down next to her and Shelley climbed into his lap. "Everything seems to be going O.K. How long before Nancy leaves?"

"Five minutes. I should go and help her make sure those two go to the bathroom before they set off."

Thomas hugged Shelley to him as he watched her go. She was an incredible young woman. He wondered for the hundredth time if she would be able to handle the group once he had gone to God.

He thought it an unfair question. There certainly was no one more capable. He was sure that under her leadership the group would do well. He was simply being selfish. He wasn't ready to die. He would have to come to terms with that fact. There was simply no choice in the matter.

He would have to go to God and he would have to do it bravely. He would set the right example for the other kids. It was part of his responsibility as the leader that they saw it as the right thing to do. It was the one thing he wondered if Josie were truly ready to have to do.

Chapter Six

Michelle stared out the window of her apartment at the dark night. She felt so lonely tonight. The nightmares had already started and she just didn't see the sense in trying to lie back down. She knew that she wouldn't be able to sleep.

She leafed through the papers covering her coffee table. They all had articles about how the dead body was found. She had decided to keep a scrapbook on the case.

Her name had been kept out of the papers so far. She didn't really care one way or another but the police had suggested that it would be for the best. Just in case they had a serial killer on the loose, they would not want who had found the girl on the front page. Just in case.

Michelle frowned, there were a lot of that in her life lately - just in case's. Lots of uncertainties, she had begun to question everything around her.

Frank said that after being that close to death, it was a normal reaction to have. Her surfer cop had not called her back yet.

She knew that it was wrong to pry anyway. The woman on the phone had assured her that he was very busy but he would call as soon as he could.

She wanted to know what they'd found.

The last thing that she'd heard was that there was no physical ID on the girl's body. Michelle could have guessed that. She was nude.

She kept thinking of how hard it had to be on the girl's parents, wherever they might be. What a way to find out that your little girl was gone.

Michelle fingered the photo album that she had brought at the drug store earlier on one of her few trips out of the apartment. She intended to clip all of the articles that she could find.

She had grown paranoid about being out of the apartment. She would never again take the short cut through the park. She had taken the long way around today to the grocery and drug stores. She had not been to work since the day before she had found the dead girl.

She sat the photo album down and decided to go in the kitchen and grab the scissors when the phone rang.

She looked at the clock on the mantle. Who would be calling here at three in the morning? It had to be Frank.

Michelle picked up on the second ring. "Hello?"

"Hi Michelle, it's Frank. Sorry to be calling back so late but the operator said that you sounded urgent. Everything all right?"

"Everything is fine." She quickly reassured him. "I was just wondering if you'd found out who she was."

Frank's end went silent for a minute. "You know that I can't tell you anything about that Michelle. It's police business now."

Michelle frowned at the receiver. "I was just curious Frank. I have the weirdest feeling about all of this. I would really like to know what happened. I can't eat or sleep anymore. I can't explain it. It's become really important to me to know who she is, to understand what happened."

Frank hesitated again. "Are you up for awhile?"

"Yeah, I can't sleep."

"I'll come by then. I should be out of here in about ten minutes. Should I bring some coffee?

We can talk, all right?"

"I just put on a fresh pot." She agreed.

Michelle hung up the phone and went in to check the coffee. Lucky that she had chanced the trip to the store. She put some hot rolls in the oven before heading in to change out of her nightgown into shorts and a T-shirt.

She headed for the bathroom deciding that quick brush of her hair and a bit of make-up would be sufficient to make her presentable.

She wasn't out to impress the cop; she simply wanted the information that only he could give her.

She studied her reflection in the bathroom mirror. Not bad. Okay, it wouldn't hurt for her to look good for the cop. It's not like he wasn't attractive.

The knock on the door brought her back to reality.

She hurried to unlock the door and pull Frank inside.

He grinned at her. "Kind of weird seeing a lady so put together this time of night. I mean, unless you're the type that works these hours."

Michelle smiled back. "Come on in. The coffee's ready. We can sit at the table in the kitchen."

"All right by me. What is that smell?"

Michelle had forgotten the rolls in the oven. She hurried in to get them and he wandered in the direction of the coffee table and all the papers stacked there. They were all stories about the girl.

He shook his head and moved into the kitchen doorway. "You are really obsessed about this thing, aren't you?"

Michelle looked up from the pan she was carrying and nodded her head. "I don't know what it is. I just can't think of anything else."

Frank watched her closely as she took the rolls off of the pan and placed them on a plate. She went to the frig and grabbed butter and coffee cream as she beckoned for him to sit.

"This is a cute little place you have here."

"It's O.K. I would like to live in a safer neighborhood. Especially now."

"Yeah, I can see that. Remember though, no matter where you live, there are bound to be draw backs." He gestured to the window. "Have you been out since you found her?"

Michelle shook her head. "Not much. I did a bit of shopping today. Does that count?"

Frank threw back his head and laughed. "I suppose that it does. What about work?"

"I haven't been to work since the day before I found the girl. I took a sick leave."

Frank helped himself to a roll, deep in thought. He could tell how deeply she had been affected by all of this. Maybe if he let her know what they had come up with, she would relax.

He turned to her with a questioning gaze. "I am sitting here wondering how much I should tell you."

She stared at him for a moment. "No matter what it is, thank God you are honest. How much do you know?"

"We found her parents."

Michelle leaned forward. "Yes, tell me about her parents.

Frank shrugged his shoulders. "Not much to tell, really." He studied her tense frame closely before continuing. "Her mother is doing time for drug possession and we still aren't sure of the situation with the father."

"Situation?" She scooted up in the chair and placed both of her tiny, perfect hands on the coffee cup.

"There were reports of sexual abuse by the father at both the schools and a hospital. We still have not actually had an interview with him."

"Do you think he had anything to do with all of this?"

"Doubtful. His current address is Florida. He's driving an ice cream truck. He reported to work the day before and the day of the murder."

Michelle searched his face as he grew quiet. "What is her name? I don't know why it's so important, but it is. I have to know her name."

Frank returned her stare for a moment before looking down to the fingers clenched so tightly around the cup. "Carrie Dawson. She turned sixteen years old the day that you found her."

Michelle stared at him in silence, letting tears run down her face. "What else do you know about her?"

"She was in and out of foster homes most of the first eight years of her life. Her mother spent most of her time on drugs or doing time for drugs and the father has never been around much, which is good as he's a known sexual offender." He frowned, wondering how much more he should say. "It seems that she was placed the last time eight years ago and ran away. There are no records of her since. The mother claims that she's had no contact and I am sure the story will be much the same with dear old dad."

Michelle nodded, brushing the tears away roughly. "Go on."

"That's really about it. We are still trying to set up the interviews with both parents. We will locate the father to find out what he knows, if anything."

Michelle stared at her cup. "Thank you. I know that you are not supposed to tell me anything. If it's any consolation I feel better just knowing her name. It's so sad in a way, isn't it?"

Frank nodded his head in agreement. If there were anything that he could do to make this pretty little lady sleep better at night, he would do it. He looked at her and smiled.

She smiled back through her tears. "It sounds in a way though, as if she is almost better off where she is now. At least she's safe."

Frank stared at her in wonder. It was a hell of a thing to say, but she had an excellent point. The poor girl had obviously led a life of sheer hell and that was just the paper work of it.

The two sat across from each other at the table, contemplating what the young dead girl named Carrie must have lived through. They both looked at each other at the same instant and smiled.

Whatever happened now, they both agreed that she had gone to a better place. It was up to people like them to figure out the rest.

Chapter Seven

Considering what they had been through the last three days, this was nothing. Thomas winced at the idea of what he would normally consider a major catastrophe being nothing now. The past few days had left him exhausted.

Most of his little band sat on the ground in various lounging positions half asleep. They had to stay here for the night, maybe longer. There was no doubt about it.

He looked over to where Josie curled up with Emily tight against her. Even she had lost her usual bounce.

Thomas dreaded the thought of staying in East Peoria for any longer than necessary. It had become painfully obvious, however, that they would need a great deal of rest and supplies before moving on. They had noticed several squad cars on the way up the hill to the park from the railroad tracks. They most certainly didn't need that kind of trouble.

He had no choice but to send John and Tracy back out for supplies. They had managed the trip from Chicago fairly well, but the trip had taken its toll on the food stores.

He went over to where the pair lay bundled against a tree under a sleeping bag. He knelt down, gently shaking Tracy's shoulder.

Tracy sat up instantly, waking John at the same time. "What's up?" she mumbled sleepily, rubbing at her eyes.

Thomas watched her trying to get herself together with a find smile. "I need the two of you to go for supplies. You don't need a list, we need everything that you can get."

John groaned and sat up. "We need to find Shelley some shoes."

Thomas grimaced, thinking of how cold it was and that the poor girl was suffering with her feet crammed into a pair of tennis shoes that were two sizes too small. If you can manage somehow, do it, but it's not priority. I'm hoping that we can board a train heading for Kansas City in two nights. We have to have food and water. Lots of it."

John simply nodded his understanding and got to his feet, stretching. "Do you mind if we take a third. Steven would be a big help."

Thomas frowned, looking to where the boy sat propped against a tree. He should really let him go. The problem was that Steven did not come even close to resembling the other two. He had dark, almost black hair and eyes of the same color.

Thomas nodded his head. Even though they looked nothing alike he knew that Steven would be useful. He had gotten the feeling that he felt inferior when talking to Wes. Maybe this would be good for his moral.

Thomas walked in front of him and knelt back down. Steven was half asleep but as soon as Thomas knelt down his eyes flew open. "Everything okay Thomas?"

"Yes, fine. I was just wondering if you would run on a supply trip with John and Tracy. They will hopefully need help hauling things back."

Steven jumped to his feet. "Of course, I will be glad to go."

Thomas grinned at his enthusiasm. "Do whatever John and Tracy ask you to do. John's in charge."

Steven dipped his head obligingly. "Of course. I'll do my best."

Thomas left him to clean up a bit and told him to bring the other two over before they left.

Steven ambled off in the direction of the blond pair, making their contrasting looks all the more apparent. He hoped that he had done the right thing.

Thomas stopped in front of Josie and Emily. "I need to talk to you for a minute Josie. Why don't you take Emily to Nan?"

"O.K. I'll be over there in a minute." Josie smiled weakly.

Thomas went over to where he had his paperwork. He picked up a few pieces and scanned the map quickly before Josie appeared at his side.

"Watcha need?" She grinned amiably.

"We need to go ahead and set up camp for tonight. I want you, Nancy and Wes to work on it with the little ones. It's going to take me some time to weed through this mess and decide exactly where we should head for."

Josie nodded understanding. "Where would you like us to set up?"

"I figure thirty feet back into those trees should be good enough cover, don't you?"

"It will be fine for the overnight. There shouldn't be much activity as cold as it is."

Thomas smiled. "That's what I am hoping for. Do you think that you can manage it within the hour? That way whoever wants to can bed down in the tent. It will be nice to get away from all of the snow."

"Definitely. Everyone wants to rest anyway. This will be good incentive. I can put Steven and Wes on the big tent. They can get it up in about twenty minutes."

Thomas shook his head. "You'll have to manage without Steven, he's going with Tracy and John."

Josie eyed him questioningly, saying nothing. She was just staring at him like he was nuts.

"What?" he finally asked her. "Is there a problem that I don't know about?"

"No, I just didn't figure on you sending Steven with John and Tracy."

"Why not?"

"Well, his asthma's been acting up for one but the main one is that the three of them look nothing alike."

Thomas frowned at her. "I know that. I think that it will work out just fine."

Josie shrugged her shoulders. "Whatever you decide Tom. You are still in charge, right?"

"Yes, Josie, I most certainly am." He studied her expression closely to see if she were being a smart ass. "However, if you think that I'm making a poor judgment, I'd be glad to listen."

Josie shook her head and stared at the ground. "Never mind Thomas. You know what's best."

"Well, I'd like to think so."

Josie spun and headed off to start the moving of the camp. It would not take real long for some of them to set up so that everyone could get some rest as comfortably as possible.

Thomas couldn't wait to head south were the weather was warmer. He hated having to move so slowly in the cold. He was more than ready for some warm weather and relaxation.

He wondered about Josie's little display of temperament. Was she getting too big for her britches? He would have to deal with that when they got south, no time for it right now.

He pushed his thoughts of Josie and the journey south aside as the three approached ready for the supply trip. It struck him again how completely opposite they were in looks.

They would be fine, he reassured himself. It was during the day, a small town. They would look like buddies, just hanging out.

Chapter Eight

The trio headed down the hill from the park in total silence. They were each lost in their own thoughts.

Steven was wondering what had made Thomas decide to send him this morning.

John worried about finding Shelley the right pair of shoes.

Tracy tried to decide where they should go first. She grabbed both boys by the arms and pulled them to a small pavilion covered in snow at the crest of the hill. "Let's format some sort of plan before we get any further."

The three headed over and took seats on the picnic tables that were inside.

Tracy squinted her eyes against the midday sun. "Is this a weekday?"

Steven and John looked at each other and nodded simultaneously that it was.

"In that case, we had better stay out of sight until around three. That's about the time that school lets out." She looked at the other two.

"Any suggestions on how we spend our time until then?"

John shook his head negatively. "I'm not familiar with this area. Are either of you?"

Steven nodded his head. "I've been here a few times when I was a kid. I have an aunt that lives nearby."

"How far?"

"I'm not real sure. It's on Meadows."

"Do you remember where the house is?" queried John.

"Yeah. It's just getting there from here. I'm not sure which way to go."

"No problem," Tracy grinned, "I saw a gas station that's not too far."

Steven eyed the two of them curiously.

John chuckled at their luck. "Good idea. Do you know what size shoes your aunt wears?"

Steven frowned, even more confused. "No, I haven't seen her in a long time."

Tracy shrugged her shoulders. "No matter. Let's get to it."

"Cool." John grabbed Steven by the shoulders, giving him a gentle pat. "Just relax. Tracy and I are pros."

Steven allowed a grin to spread across his face. "That's what I am afraid of."

The trio sat off laughing.

Tracy went into the gas station and found that Meadows was but three quarters of a mile in the other direction. They could take side streets for most of the way there and it wasn't far from the high school, a definite plus.

When it was time for school to be out they would blend easily as students.

They were all more confident that they had a plan.

They were only four blocks down Meadows when Steven recognized a nice sized corner house as his aunt's.

They walked around the block, checking for cars or signs of a pet. Finding neither, they went to the back of the house. They checked for windows and doors that might be ajar. Again, they found nothing.

John shrugged his shoulders and looked at Tracy. She pulled a gas credit card that she had taken from the station. She applied it to the back door.

They were soon rewarded with the door popping open.

Tracy grinned at the other two, gesturing grandly for them to enter.

The three split up, maintaining complete silence. Tracy headed for the kitchen, Steven and John for the bedrooms.

The rule was that they were to be in and out of the house in ten minutes, just in case.

When the ten minutes were up, the three met back in the kitchen with their arms full.

Tracy had found a bunch of plastic shopping bags under the sink. They crammed their findings into the bags. It would make for easier hauling, without attracting much attention.

John grinned as he stuffed the three pairs of tennis shoes he had found into a bag. He felt sure that one of the three would fit Shelley.

The three hurried out of the house, leaving by the back yard. They kept to the side streets, heading in the opposite direction from where they had come.

When they reached the bottom of the hill that headed into the park, Steven stopped and stared at the other two. "Do you mean to tell me that all of the stuff that we use is stolen?"

John and Tracy looked at each other for a second. They had known that this was coming.

Tracy decided to do the talking. "Some of the time it is. There are times when we can work but those are few and far between. It's mostly times like this when we are short on a lot of things and have to move soon.

John pulled Steven to walking again. "We are going to have to hit the neighborhood grocery store after we drop this first load off. If you don't want to come back out with us, you don't have to. It's the way that we have to do things in order to survive."

Steven nodded understanding. He didn't like it, but he accepted it as the way things had to be. "Hey, I'm just dying to see what happens at the grocery store."

John smiled, knowing that they had won him over. "If it makes you feel any better, your aunt had a nice home owner's insurance policy. I'm pretty sure that she will be compensated."

Steven shrugged his shoulders. He was out

of breath from talking anyway.

He wondered if it would have stopped them if she didn't. Probably not.

They were quiet until they reached the top of the hill near the camp. John explained that they would drop this load off and head right back out.

Tracy grimaced, holding out the four bags that she carried. "This isn't enough groceries to last us for a day. We have to hit the store."

After they had found the camp's new spot and left the bags with Josie, they headed right back down the hill.

"There's a grocery store just at the bottom of the hill and to the left. We should go ahead and hit there. If we do fairly well, we may be finished for the day."

John patted her affectionately on the shoulder. "You realize, of course, that the woman is in charge, not me."

The three had a good laugh as they headed for the store. They swung down a side street and passed a big yellow house with a huge back yard. No one was home.

This they would establish as base. John and Tracy explained that they would go to the front of the grocery store and "hang out".

When some one came out with a cart full, they would grab a bag while the customer was loading and calmly walk the other way.

It sounded simple, but wasn't. If you wanted to work the same grocery store for a while, you couldn't be seen. They usually worked as a team, passing the bag to the other person and just walking away, as if they had come from the store themselves.

They would then walk around the block, drop off the bags at base and do it all over again.

They decided that they would work as a team, two going to the front of the store, the third remaining with the stash of bags. The third would rotate off so that there were fresh faces and they would all get a chance to "grab".

The other two decided that Steven needed the practice. He did very well.

After a couple of hours at the first store and several trips up the hill with their loads in between, they found another grocery and department store just across the highway.

Between the three locations they managed very well indeed. There were twenty-three trips up and down the hill of the park before nightfall.

Josie and Tracy inventoried and decided that they had done so well that they were in good shape for several days on the train.

Steven still felt guilty about what they were doing. He knew that John and Tracy had a good point in that they needed the things that they took. It didn't stop him from feeling the pangs of knowing that you were doing something wrong.

Tracy eyed him from time to time, wondering what he was thinking. Would he want to go with them again? He had been a great help today.

John was exhausted, but happy. Two of the three pairs of shoes fit Shelley.

Chapter Nine

Thomas studied the hills that rolled gently past the open door of the freight car. They had finally had a stroke of luck. The train that they had hopped in East Peoria had put their car off the main in Galesburg.

A mutual decision by Josie and himself decided that they would stay with the cars. Even if they weren't picked up and headed south the entire group needed the rest. They were still exhausted.

The cars were picked back up without being checked and now seemed to be headed southwest. Thomas was trying to determine exactly where they were when Emily came over to tug on his shirt. "I'm hungry Thomas."

He grinned down at the little beauty. "Let's go and see what there is to munch on sweetie."

He picked the three-year-old up and carefully crossed the moving freight car. He sat her down in front of Josie. "Have we got something that this little lady can snack on?"

Josie patted the little girl affectionately on the

head. "Well, let me see," she grinned at the child. "How about a cookie? But only if you pass out two to everybody."

Emily bobbed her head, "Sure."

Josie handed the cookies over after opening them.

Emily made her way across the freight car on wobbly legs doling out cookies as she went.

Thomas dropped down next to Josie and draped his arm around her shoulders, giving her a tight squeeze.

She leaned into the embrace enjoying the feeling of friendship that seemed so far behind them now. "Where do you think that we are headed?"

"I'd say that we are headed towards Kansas City. I'm not positive but the direction we are traveling and the time we've been riding, it's a guess. The terrain looks like Missouri."

Josie studied the may that he pulled from his pocket and unfolded. He was right. From what she could see, they were headed straight for Kansas City. "Are we getting off there?"

"I think it would be best. I'd like us to head over to Wichita from there. We need to head in the general direction of California over the next few weeks. The first week of November is creeping up pretty fast. I, or should I say we, have to be there no later than the seventh for the meeting of group leaders." He gave her another squeeze.

"I'm still kind of nervous about that Thomas. What's it like?"

Thomas hesitated, not wanting to tell her more than she needed to know for right now. There would be enough all at once when the time came. Why not try and keep the blow soft? "Just don't worry about that all too much. We'll deal with it when the time comes, O.K."

Josie managed a weak smile in response. He certainly wasn't going to tell her anything. She pulled away from him.

He eyed her uncomfortably. He must have given her the wrong impression again. Not knowing what else he should say, he shrugged his shoulders and stood back up. "Why don't you prepare the children to disembark? I think that if my guess is correct, we'll be stopping soon."

Josie gladly moved away from him and went to get the others organized.

Thomas watched her stiff back and winced. He couldn't seem to say the right thing, especially here lately. He and Josie used to be so close. They were the best of friends. Why did it have to be this way? Was it because that she were training to take his spot? Did it make her uncomfortable knowing that he was going to God?

He thought back to the time just before her brother Patrick had gone. She hadn't acted this way when Patrick had gone. What was the difference?

Thomas shrugged his shoulders again, grinning at Lil' Dawne who was ambling in his direction.

She stretched out her arms to be picked up.

Thomas grabbed her up and slung her onto his hip, giving her back a rub. "Whatcha need little one?"

Lil' Dawne eyed him tearfully. "Josie says that I have to go potty in the bucket again and I don't want to."

"Well, honey, we have to get off the train soon. We'll have to hurry away from the tracks so there won't be time for you to go potty for awhile after we get off. You really should go now."

"O.K. if you say I have to but I'm not going to like it. Everybody can see you when you do it that way."

"How about I come over and hold a blanket up so that nobody can see? Would that make it better?"

The child nodded her head eagerly and Thomas sat her down.

He followed her and kept his word under the wary gaze of Josie.

Josie turned away to tend to Kevin and Darryl, who were unhappy about having to put on their shoes. How would she ever manage without him? Would she be able to take care of all of these kids with the same love and understanding that he did?

She turned from helping feisty little Darryl with his shoes to find Thomas staring at her.

He headed over to stand next to her. "Do you have anything specific that you would like me to do?"

She gestured over to Emily, who now lay sound asleep clutching her cookie in Nancy's lap. "You could grab her so that Nancy can get her things together."

Thomas went over and picked up the child. He returned, carefully holding onto her so that she still slept. "Are you O.K. Josie? I really worry about you sometimes."

Josie shrugged her shoulders. "I just feel like I can't talk to you the way that I used to Thomas. I'm scared at the idea of being in charge of everything."

Thomas freed an arm from Emily to pull Josie next to him. "I would never have asked you to do it if I didn't think that you could handle it."

Josie snuggled into his arm, looking up at him. "Tell me I'm just being paranoid Tom."

"I can't tell you that Josie. It's going to be hard sometimes. But I am sure that you will manage. It's just going to take some getting used to."

Josie pulled away from him to grab at Kevin who was about to topple over with the sway of the train. He still did not have his shoes on right.

Thomas pulled Emily closer into his arms, dreading the thought of waking her.

He watched Josie pick Kevin up and set him on her hip. After his shoes were straightened out, she made her way over to help Shelley with her new shoes.

How could a person with so much love to give ever fail?

Chapter Ten

The group made it off the train and was headed for the park less than an hour after Thomas had Josie pack them up. They had decided that they would camp in a large park on the outskirts of Kansas City before heading on towards Wichita.

Once they reached the camp, they discovered several hunters milling about, in spite of the off-season. It seemed they were shooting rabbits.

Of course it was illegal to hunt the furry little creatures in the off-season but it seemed especially barbaric to have these men doing it just for the entertainment.

It was one thing to hunt for food; it was another to hunt for pleasure. The group saw no pleasure in taking another life, even animal life, just for kicks.

They decided to push on and headed about three hundred yards further into deep tree cover before Thomas felt comfortable about setting up camp.

He sent Wes, John, Darryl and Steven into the

woods to do a quick scout of the area.

He nominated Nancy and Tracy to set up the main tent.

When these two things were set into motion he beckoned to Josie and the two discussed what they would need for supplies before continuing on to Wichita.

By the time the pair had finished the supply list the others had returned from their scouting. They reported seeing no one within five hundred yards of the perimeter. Wes also suggested they post guards, just in case.

Thomas agreed and they sent two pairs into the trees. He sent Wes and Steven to the right and Darryl and John to the left.

After establishing base camp Thomas called on Tracy and Nancy to head out for supplies. They were to go with Josie and had explicit directions to be back no later than an hour after nightfall. He wanted them to get water and drinking supplies more than anything. They were almost completely sapped on water. He would like to see them come up with enough for at least the little ones to take a bath. He wanted them to clean up some before they headed to Kansas.

Once Thomas had sent all the parties on their way, he gathered the small ones in front of the main tent. "O.K. you guys. I need a hand. Kevin and Shelley, I want the two of you to find some big rocks. As big as you can carry and bring them back here. Don't wander too far from here though, got it?"

The pair obligingly set off chattering excitedly.

Lil' Dawne came to stand in from of him. "Do you have stuff for me to help?"

"Yep, I certainly do. I want you to dig in the snow." He pointed to the center of the clearing in front of the big tent. "Here's my work gloves. I know they are too big but they'll have to do for now."

Lil' Dawne grinned ear to ear. It sure didn't seem like much of a job to have to dig in the snow.

Thomas went over to where Emily still sat in her sled. "Would you mind sharing your sled with some wood for a fire?"

Thomas got his answer from the adoring smile that she beamed up at him. Ah, it was good to be loved.

He towed Emily in her sled behind him and went from tree to tree, pulling select branches down to his reach. He hacked them off with his bow knife. The entire group would love to have a good hot meal and a warm fire for a change. It would be a great boost for morale.

After filling Emily's sled to the point where there was only room left for her, he headed over to inspect Lil' Dawne's work. She had a nice sized hole dug clear through to the dirt. Just what he needed and she grinned when he told her so.

Thomas grabbed a bunch of twigs that were the driest and massed them in the center. He grabbed a tallow candle from his pack. He added a wad of newspaper. He lit the candle in the center and continued to add twigs until the fire took a firm hold, the flames growing stronger and stronger.

Emily sat in the sled next to him, eyeing the blaze with interest.

After being sure that the fire would stay lit he went back and started to gather more wood.

By the time he had arrived with another load, Kevin and Shelley had a great pile of rocks near the fire. With their help, they encircled the fire with rocks. With what was left over they built a large pile that they would use for cooking purposes later.

Thomas took Kevin and Shelley with him and continued to gather firewood until he had a stack that he was confidant would last them through the night. He left Emily with Lil' Dawne with strict instructions not to let the baby too close to the fire.

On the last trip back Thomas had the other two grab a couple of huge felled logs that he'd noticed earlier. They drug them back through the snow and Lil' Dawne and Emily brushed them clean. Together they pushed them close to the fire where they would dry.

Thomas grinned at all they had accomplished and headed his little ones into the big tent to round up some lunch. He felt as though he could eat a horse.

Just when he'd gotten the other children fed and sat down with a sandwich of his own, the three girls reappeared, carrying several jugs of water.

Josie said that they had found an out building in the park that was an hour's walk away. They could tap all the water they would need right there.

Thomas patted Josie on the back. They decided that they would go ahead and get baths for the little ones while he took the sled and the jugs and went for more.

The three older girls dug through the backpacks of supplies for soap, shampoo, conditioner and a few bath toys.

They sat the huge tub over the fire outside and filled it to the brim. All of the emptied jugs were put into Thomas sled and he headed for the water after getting directions from Josie.

After he left, the girls built another fire close to the entrance to the tent. They got out fresh cloths for Emily and Kevin, who were to be the first and carried the hot water from one big tub to the other in pails.

Emily readily stripped and dived in while the rest of the group watched her in obvious delight. She squealed at the bath toys they had found her and fussed when Josie and Tracy attacked at the same time with soap and shampoo.

The group went on with baths in this fashion until even the boys out on watch had been relieved and came in for their turns in the tub.

After the last of the bath things were dried off and put away they made a dinner of Thomas's hardy beef stew with bread and potatoes.

They sat around the campfire with full stomachs and tired eyes until Josie started putting the younger ones in beds in various tents around the campfire.

After everyone had made their way to a pallet or sleeping bag, Josie and Thomas headed for the big tent.

They had yet to decide how long they would stay here and which direction they would take from here.

The two talked and argued over the map until the wee hours of the morn, finally deciding that they would head for Wichita in three days, on foot.

They both knew that the journey would not be an easy one but they thought that three days would give everyone adequate time to rest and relax.

They needed everybody to be in good shape before they headed out of the state on foot. It would be one hell of a trip, but they were headed for warmer weather and the yearly meeting. Surely that would give them enough inspiration to make the journey go as well as possible.

Thomas and Josie curled up in a sleeping bag together. They both said it was for warmth. They both knew it was for security. They needed each other. How would they ever manage alone?

Chapter Eleven

Emily let out a high pitched wail and was quickly silenced by Josie's hand over her mouth. "Not now baby girl. You can scream all you want, as loud as you want when we break for camp. But just not now O.K."

Emily eyed her tearfully but nodded her head.

Josie squinted against the dark night, trying to locate Thomas. It was time for him to take over the small charge. Her patience was about shot. She needed to be alone for a bit. She needed some space and time to think.

Josie balanced Emily on her hip and jogged, catching up to John, Tracy and Steven. "Can you three control this one while I find Thomas?"

Tracy nodded her head and took the little one into her arms carefully.

Steven grabbed Josie's elbow and pulled her close. He whispered into her ear. "I think he's up with Shelley and Kevin both in the sled. We had some trouble with Kevin earlier and turned him over to Thomas."

Josie frowned in the dark. "Could you three handle Shelley if I bring her back and trade for Emily?"

John nodded wearily. "I think Shelley would be O.K. with me for awhile."

"Great." Josie answered and headed off at a trot. She came across Thomas about thirty feet in front of everyone else, with the exception of Wes, who was advanced as lookout.

He looked up at her approach and she noticed how drained he looked. Thomas always shouldered more of his share than anyone else.

Shelley and Kevin were wrapped together in the sled sound asleep. "How long have they been out?" Josie asked.

"About twenty minutes. I had a hell of a time with Kevin. He's been having nightmares again."

"Great. Well, why don't you let me take the sled back to Tracy, John and Steven? You look like you could use a break."

Thomas wearily shook his head no. "If Kevin wakes up, I want to be right here with him."

Josie eyed him tiredly. She was in no mood to

argue with this obstinate moron. She knew, as he did, that if he wore himself out the entire group was at risk.

Josie silently matched his pace for a while in silence. She grabbed one of the pull straps from his gloved hand and pulled right along next to him. With Kevin and Shelley both in the sled it had to weigh well over a hundred pounds.

She could already feel the pain travel across her shoulders.

"This is insane. What do you say to split them up? Let me take Shelley in the other sled. Emily's not using it. Tracy's carrying her. We can put her in the sled with Kevin and take the other one back to Tracy with Shelley in it."

Thomas thought about it for a second before nodding his agreement. Shelley would be just fine with her hero, John. "Where's Lil' Dawne?"

"She's with Nancy. She's wide-awake and walking. She's quite the spunky one, you know."

Thomas grinned at the thought of the mouse brown head bent in concentration while digging a hole in the snow. She was a little trooper. The great part was that if she stayed awake all night, she would sleep most of the day.

The way it was now, the older kids slept in shifts, taking care of the little ones that were awake.

Josie headed off in search of the other sled. She wasn't sure who had it or what it was being used to carry. She knew that it would be worth it to find. Thomas had to take it easy or he would be worthless.

She found the sled with Nancy's group about fifty feet behind John, Tracy and Steven. The good news with them was that Emily had fallen asleep on Tracy's hip.

After she had talked Darryl into giving up the sled, she passed the packs that it carried to the others as she went past.

When she got back to where Tracy still kept her long legged pace, despite the added weight of Emily, she gave each of them a pack and placed Emily into the sled.

She stopped long enough to tuck a bundle of blankets around the sleeping child and continued at break neck speed to catch up to Thomas.

Once she'd caught up with him, she paused long enough to give him a big hug before taking Shelley from his sled.

Thomas eyed her questioningly. "What was that for?"

Josie grinned. "For being a hard headed pain in the ass."

"Why's that?"

"Because, even at times like this, you think of everyone else."

He shrugged his shoulders nonchalantly. "It's what's expected of me Josie. Someday the responsibility to care for all these babes will be yours."

Josie didn't respond. It was almost four in the morning and they would have to stop and take cover before first light. She didn't want to take the time to try and explain her insecurities right now. It just didn't seem appropriate. There would be time enough to discuss all that when they set on a sight for camping in Wichita.

Josie didn't reply at all, she just stepped away pulling the sled with Shelley in it to a halt. She would wait here to turn over the sled to John and take the opportunity to catch her breath.

She stood silently watching the others draw near, smiling as they went by.

Nancy, a pack strapped to her back with the

small hands of Lil' Dawn and Darryl in her big soft ones on either side, smiled back and kept moving at a good pace.

Lil' Dawne looked up just long enough to grin at her for a quick flash before returning her concentration to the ground.

Darryl with his soft brown hair flowing out behind him, looked at everything but the ground in front of him. He smiled as he stumbled along, Nancy's firm grasp on him keeping him on his feet.

A few minutes later, John, Steven and Tracy came into sight. John came over and grabbed the sled with Shelley in it from Josie taking the time to give her a rub on the shoulder. "Don't worry. She'll be safe with me."

"I know she will John." She smiled down at the still sleeping nine -year old.

She stood still for another moment, watching Tracy place Emily in the sled next to Shelley and the threesome each grabbing a pull strap. They walked arm in arm pulling the sled behind them.

It was a wonder that the blue-eyed angels were the best thieves in the group.

Once more Josie reminded herself that it was

a necessary evil. Besides, she would rather have those two on her side any day.

Josie hurried to catch up to them and put her arm through Steven's, who was ambling along casually. She matched his pace for a while. There was something special about Steven, with his dark good looks and quiet nature. He was one of her favorites.

Of course, they were all something special, weren't they? Each and every one of them had something special to offer that made the group whole.

The way things were now they were a great family. They were all a part of the best family that they had ever known.

They would always be together, until death, one way or another.

Chapter Twelve

Thomas sighed and rubbed his eyes before returning his stare to the map spread before him on his quilt. As far as he could tell they were on the John Redmond Reservation, near the Neosho River.

He grinned, feeling stupid. He knew that they were near the river. That was why they had stopped early last night. They had camped about 700 feet from a stream that Wes had found scouting.

Thomas's grin quickly changed back to a frown. They still had a long way to go. If he was guessing fairly accurately, they were still at least a hundred miles to Wichita.

His gaze wandered from the map to look around the camp. Steven, who had some trouble breathing last night, was sitting, half asleep, propped against a tree.

Thomas pulled himself to his feet and put his map away. He grabbed his quilt and went to cover the hard working young man.

Thomas sank to the ground in front of Steven

and let his weary gaze travel over all of his kids. The only one awake besides him was Emily. She was coloring a picture that Josie had given her to keep her out of mischief. Josie had headed for a nearby tree and was curled up fast asleep.

Thomas went over and knelt beside Emily. "That's a pretty picture you're coloring, sweetie."

Emily smiled up at him. "Pretty, yes. It's for you."

"Why thank you little one. I'll keep it forever."

He went back over where Steven was now sound asleep sitting up. His pack was there and he wanted to put the picture in it for safekeeping.

After tucking the picture in his bag, he grabbed Emily's tiny hand and led her to where the food was packed. He was supposed to start their main meal at around two in the afternoon. It was one thirty now.

He quickly decided on lunch meat and cheese. They would have to go easy on the bread and chips. There wasn't much else to choose from. They would have to do something about a supply run soon.

After he had gotten all of the food prepared

he sent Emily around to wake the others.

Emily went from person to person and whispered in their ears that it was time to get up and eat. Most of them woke without further prodding. She let Josie sleep, as he had asked her to since she'd just lain down.

After he had doled out portions for the evening meal he went over to Nancy and gave her directions on making up the packets of food for the night's hike.

While he was still talking with her, John and Tracy came over. When he'd finished with Nancy, the pair offered to take over with Emily so that he could sleep awhile.

Thomas gladly accepted the offer and went over to his pack. Before he could sleep he would have to decide on their course for the nights travel.

It wasn't difficult. He decided that they would follow the river to where it met with Highway 54. They would walk along the edge of the woods and fields running parallel until they came to a small town bordering the highway. There they would take the time to send a group in for supplies.

They would have to make camp no more than

15 or 20 minutes from the town to enable supply runs. It would depend on the size of the town.

It seemed that if the town were too small there were too many folks who noticed them and might interfere. The fairly large towns at least offered a feeling of being anonymous. You could also be sure of a larger number of school age children with which they would blend.

Thomas marked his plan out in red and set it aside. It was very important that they mark everything as far as their group's movements. At the chapter meeting that they were headed for in Utah, they would make copies of the maps that they used over the course of the year and exchange them. The copy given to all of the leaders would help to ensure that no route were repeated, especially those routes taken and used when a child went to God. These areas were usually left alone for at least five years. They were never to repeat a visit to the same spot two years in a row.

Thomas had broken both of these rules.

Ever since Nancy had joined the group five years earlier, they had visited the same spot over and over again. Nancy had been pregnant when she joined the group. They had been on the outskirts of Denver, near the Arapaho

National Park, when they had come across the young girl, already having labor pains.

She had run away when she found out that she was pregnant. Her father had molested her. Nancy was afraid that if either one of her parents found out that she were with child because of it, the consequences would be unbearable.

Thomas, Josie and Wes helped deliver the baby. They cared for Nancy and the child for the next three weeks as best they could. By the end of the third week there had been more rules broken and it was time to move on.

By mutual decision by Josie and Nancy, they decided the best way to handle the baby was to try and find her a normal home. They would try and find suitable parents and leave her with them. Why not offer the child a shot a normalcy. There were still decent people out there, right?

They had accomplished this with a young couple in Aurora, Colorado. There was a listing agency for adoptions that ran ads for the couple. The group simply tailed them home.

Thomas allowed the group a month of keeping an eye on the young couple for any abnormalities. After a long discussion with Josie and Nancy, the three of them decided that it was worth a try with Matt and Darby. They left the baby girl on the doorstep with supplies, of course. The note left with the child explained that the mother had been a runaway unable to provide care for it.

The couple worked out the rest and kept the baby without further ado.

Since Nancy had joined the group, they headed for Aurora on November 6th. They would not have any contact with her, though Nancy had long ago explained who she was to Matt and Darby. They would simply follow the three around as they went shopping or to the park. The entire family had grown to know them and would take turns going in to see her.

Since the group had brought her into the world and her mother was one of them, they considered her theirs. It happened the same way with Emily, though she was with them all of the time.

The thing that concerned Thomas with the group was how it would be handled when he would go to God. This would be his last year of getting to see the child.

He pushed away the achy feeling that came with knowing that next year at this time he would not be here. He would not see the little girl named Joy that he had helped to bring into the world. He would not see Emily grow into the beauty that she was sure to become. He would not see Steven regain his confidence and win his battle with asthma. He would not watch Josie provide the care and understanding to the children he considered his own. He would be going to God.

Chapter Thirteen

Frank listened to the ringing phone that still wasn't being answered. He grimaced and slammed the receiver back into the cradle on his desk. He had been trying for three days to get a hold of Michelle.

A number of thoughts began to race through his mind. He wondered if she had something major go wrong. He knew that she had quit her job the week before.

He shook his head and gathered up the paperwork that littered his desk. He would finish straightening his mess and head to her apartment.

He let a deep chuckle roll from the back of his throat. He would buy supplies and camp on her doorstep until she returned. He had the next day off. He had nowhere else to be. He really felt like he needed to see her.

Ever since their conversation at the apartment three weeks ago, they had kept in constant contact. He had gone back over to her place a few times, then to dinner. They had talked to each other on the phone every day.

He had thought that they were developing some sort of on-going relationship. Now what in the hell was going on?

He was beginning to wish that he had never gone there in the first place. Cops and relationships just didn't mix. Everyone knew that. He had thought that this would be different.

He could kick himself for discussing the Dawson case with her. It had become a regular topic of conversation with the two of them. The more he thought about it the more he wondered if maybe she was just seeing him to get information.

No, he was letting his imagination run away with him. Michelle wasn't that kind of person. She wouldn't do that to him. Would she?

Frank once again shook his head with disgust and picked up the phone. He dialed the all too familiar number and let it ring ten times before hanging back up.

He piled all of the papers neatly in one spot, deciding that he couldn't concentrate anyway. He would come in tomorrow and finish his reports up on his day off.

He went to the locker room and grabbed his things. He left the bundle of papers that he usually carried with him in the top of the locker and headed for his car.

He wouldn't be able to concentrate on the case tonight either. He had gathered some information on the Dawson case and compiled his own dossier.

He and Michelle had spent a lot of time with the case file he'd developed. He had done some computer research on the case and taken the printouts over to her apartment one night.

He had come to find that she had a real knack for investigating. Between the two of them, they had come up with several possibilities that had never been mentioned before.

The detective that was handling the case didn't mind a few fresh ideas so they had met over lunch to discuss some of his theories.

At the lunch, he had found out that they finally located Carrie's father. He was remarried with two children. He had not had contact with Carrie in years.

The detective said that they had checked him out and found no reason not to believe him.

Besides this, the detective had no new information. They had already established the cause of death to be asphyxiation. There had been a few bruises and things but no tale-tell signs of a physical struggle.

Frank had a few other things that he'd wanted to add but the detective made it obvious he was more concerned with the free meal.

Frank parked his car across the street from Michelle's apartment. There were no lights on.

He shrugged and grabbed the bag from the deli he'd picked up on his way. He was in no hurry. He would wait.

He hiked up the two flights of stairs to her apartment and knocked on the door. No answer.

He sat down in the floor with a copy of the day's newspaper in front of him and got out his sandwich.

He was just getting ready to bite when an elderly man approached from the stairs. "You looking for Michelle?"

Frank nodded his head that he was.

The little old man shook his head. "Won't do you much good to be here. She moved out three days ago."

Frank stared at the old man in silence for a second while it sunk in. "You are kidding right? I just talked to her three days ago. She didn't say anything about moving."

The old man shrugged his shoulders again. "Don't know much about any of that mister. I know she seemed to be in sort of a rush. She was paid up for the month too. Kind of strange, isn't it?"

Frank just nodded his head, trying not to look upset. "By any chance did she leave a forwarding address?"

The old man eyed him for a minute before saying anything. "Come down to my apartment. I'll get it for you."

Frank smiled appreciatively. "If it makes you feel any better, I'm a cop."

The old man shrugged his shoulders. "That doesn't really mean a whole hell of a lot nowadays, does it?"

Frank attempted to laugh, which came out more like a strangled cough. "Why are you giving me her address then?"

"I've seen you here before. You seem like a decent sort of fellow. The look on your face when

I told you she moved counts a bunch. Sweet girl."

The old man went into his apartment and came back out with a name and address copied on a piece of paper. "She told me to forward all of her mail to this address. Good luck mister. Michelle was a hell of a lady."

Frank nodded his agreement. He thanked the old man profusely and headed for his car with address and deli bag firmly in hand.

He hadn't eaten all day. He took the sandwich out of its white paper and munched it quickly in the car.

He wondered what kind of shit she was trying to prove? Why would she bail on him without even a good-bye? He thought that they had something. Well, he wasn't just going to let it end like this. He would get in touch with her. One way or another.

Chapter Fourteen

Finally, they had made it. They were at a large park on the outskirts of Wichita. There was an air force base near-by. Thomas had said that he thought it was McConnell Air Force Base. Wes wasn't sure, he just knew that they could hear the planes overhead from time to time. He liked planes a lot. He wondered if he would get the opportunity to check a couple of them out while they were here.

He should have time. Thomas had said that they would stay here for a couple of weeks. Everybody needed the rest.

Thomas was certainly right about that, he thought to himself as he looked around at the others in camp. They had been on the move for twelve nights straight now. Everyone had been so glad to hear Thomas say to set up camp that a couple of the girls had actually cried. Josie had fallen asleep standing up a couple of days ago. She still had a good-sized purple-blue bruise on her forehead. She looked like hell.

As soon as they established base camp, Thomas sent John and Tracy with Steven for supplies. They were almost completely out of food from the small town they hit for supplies on Highway 54.

Wes gazed longingly up into the sky and then took a long survey of the area that he could see from his tree. He had been given first watch.

When he'd scouted the area earlier he had noticed that several of the trees in this park were useless weeping willow types. They wouldn't be able to hold a person for very long, very comfortably. He knew this from experience.

Wes had been with the group the longest. He had been with them for seven years. After Patrick, Josie's brother had gone to God; they wanted him to take over as the group's leader. He had quickly refused. He knew that he just didn't have what it took to be responsible for all of the other kids. They had let him decide on his own, which was cool, but they were all sort of shocked when he turned it down.

Wes didn't really talk a whole lot. The others, who had known him for a long time, knew this and didn't pester him about it. He just liked to keep to himself.

He wondered if it were the way the he had

been bought up in Norfolk, Virginia. His father was a Navy man. His father was also very, very strict. You were not allowed to speak unless spoken to first. You were not allowed to have bad grades. You went to bed at exactly seven thirty, even on the weekends.

Oh, he knew that he didn't have it as bad as some of the other kids, but he had grown to hate his mother and his father. He knew that if he stuck around something bad would end up happening.

His mother had never done anything to him. That was the problem. She was nice to look at, but useless, like a willow tree.

He had an older sister. Her name was Cindy. She was also very pretty, but the difference was that she took care of Wes. Cindy took care of everything in the household, even the cooking and the cleaning. The only thing that she didn't do was the shopping.

Wes's mother took care of this. He laughed out loud at the memory. She would spend four hours in the bathroom on Saturdays to get ready to go to the grocery store.

His father would sit in the chair in the kitchen, reading the paper and drinking coffee, yelling at her once in awhile to hurry the hell up.

Wes grinned. At least he had some fond memories of being at home, growing up. It wasn't like that at all with the other kids.

He was glad that he could remember all of his family with a bit of a laugh, otherwise he didn't know how he would deal with how he'd left. Knowing what he did now about the other kids, he wondered if he'd done the right thing in leaving. At the time it had seemed the only way out without hurting anybody.

He remembered going to Patrick only a few days after being with the group. He told Patrick how he'd come home with a report card that had a C- and his father had gone ballistic, telling him that those kinds of grades were unacceptable. He didn't care if Cindy's grades were lousy. She was a woman. All she had to do in life was look good to get what she needed.

Wes talked back to his father for the first and only time, telling him that Cindy had to do plenty to survive because Mom did nothing.

It was also the first and only time that his father beat him with his fists. He had punched Wes so hard that he lost the three teeth in front.

After Wes's father had beaten him black and

blue he locked him in the basement, giving both his sister and his mother strict instructions that he be given no food or water. They were not to open the door for anything.

Cindy had let him out at about three in the morning. She had packed his things and some food. She told him that the only chance he had to do any good with his life was to leave. She wouldn't explain to him why she thought that, she just told him that if he cared for her at all he would run as far as fast as he could and never come back.

He had gone. He still didn't quite understand everything that she had told him that night but the other girls in the group had talked about what their fathers had done to them.

He wondered for the millionth time if his father had done these things to Cindy. That would explain a lot of things about his life back than.

He wondered about Kevin. His father had sexually molested him. It was the reason that Kevin woke screaming in the middle of the night. He wondered if Cindy woke screaming because of their father?

Thomas said that with a lot of time and love

Kevin would eventually be able to out grow the nightmares. Wes wondered if Cindy and the others would be able to do the same. He wished that he felt in some way now that he could do right by his sister. He would never know now. He wanted to go back to Norfolk and figure out a way to see her, talk to her but knew that Thomas would never allow it.

He swore that he only wanted to know if that were the reason that his sister had begged him to leave. He thought that it would make him feel better to know if it were true or not. That would at least explain why Cindy had begged him to leave.

He wondered how she was after all this time. If she had gotten out? Gotten married? Kids? He was certain that Cindy would be an awesome Mom. She always had been to him.

He pulled his thoughts away from his sister and watched Steven approaching with John and Tracy, their arms loaded with bags. Looked as if they had done well. That was great, he was starved.

He gave a long low whistle and slid to the ground.

The trio greeted him with satisfied, though

exhausted faces. These three had not slept since camp had been set this morning. Thomas had sent them straight out for supplies.

He grabbed an armful and walked with them back to the camp without a word spoken, just shared tired smiles.

He once again thanked his lucky stars that he had turned down the leader position. He could never do what Thomas did and he knew it.

Oh, he loved everyone in the group and all, but he just didn't have what it took to maintain for everyone, he was just happy to be third in charge. He was a great scout and he loved doing it. There were other jobs that he got stuck with that he didn't much like, but that came with everything in life.

He looked up to watch Josie come forward to help with the bags and thought of his sister.

One day, before he went to God he would have his questions answered. It would be the only way that he would die in peace. That were the only way, whether Thomas liked it or not.

Chapter Fifteen

Thomas stood and walked to the center of the circle neat the small fire that was dying down from supper.

He eyed his little group and raised his hand for silence. "I would like everyone to pay close attention for the next few minutes. There are some things that I need to say. I know that everyone is still pretty tired, so I won't keep you very long."

Thomas let his smile convey his feelings as he gazed around the circle. Everyone looked full and warm for a change. It had been a very long two weeks.

He cleared his throat. "I want to congratulate all of you for your stamina over the past two weeks. They have been difficult for all of us. I want you to know how much I appreciate all that you have done."

He paused and cleared his throat again. "The matter that is bothering me are the mixed signals I've been getting regarding Carrie's going to God."

This grabbed everyone's full attention. He had been sure that it would.

"Carrie did not want to go to God. She was sure that despite all of our rules and all of the love that we'd shown her for the past several years it meant nothing. She assumed that we would admonish her for not wanting to go to God and she tried to run away." Thomas paused again to clear his throat. He looked over to where Josie sat with Emily in her lap. "Would you be a champ and go and get me something to drink?"

Josie nodded her head in compliance and took Emily with her over to the food storage area.

Thomas looked over to where Wes was sitting. "Wes saw her take off. He was on watch that night. He came and woke me and we took care of it. We did not do anything to make her think that we would harm her. I tried to tell her that we would just talk."

Thomas stopped to take a drink from the cup that Josie handed him. His gaze followed her as she went back to sit down. "Carrie wouldn't listen to me. Wes tried to talk to her too. She just wouldn't listen to him either."

He paused and shook his head, trying to stop

the tears from coming with the memory. "We were forced to send Carrie to God. I could not risk her running away and possibly going to the police. I could not put us all at risk. Does everyone understand?"

Thomas let his gaze go from one to the other in the group. No one said anything.

"I hope that you all see why I had to do what I did. I did not want to hurt Carrie. I just wanted her to come back with Wes and I and talk." The tears were flowing down his cheeks non-stop now.

Josie stood up and handed Emily to Nancy. She came round to stand next to Thomas and wrapped her arm around his shoulders. He was shaking.

Josie let her stare slide from face to face in the group around the fire. The faces were all reflecting the same emotions that Thomas was sharing with his tears. No one said a word.

Josie gestured to them one by one. "Thomas let me be the first to assure you that we understand what happened. You don't need to explain. We all know that it must have been really hard for you to do what you had to do back there. We all know that Carrie was very high strung. We all knew that she was not happy to be going to God. It's going to be alright Thomas."

Josie stopped and pointed to Wes. "Wes saw everything that happened that night, didn't you bud? He told Steven and I on the way back. There was never a need for you to explain. You did what you felt you had to do to protect the rest of us."

Wes came to stand with Thomas and Josie. "If anyone doubts that Thomas did the right thing, they can come and ask me. I'll straighten them out quick."

Josie grinned and used her other arm to hug him close.

Wes stiffened but allowed the hug, which was a wonder.

Thomas looked from one to the other gratefully. "I know that the last two weeks have been hard one all of us. I felt that I needed to clear the air now that we are settled in for a bit with a chance to talk."

Emily made her way to him, pushing Nancy's hands firmly away. She came to give Thomas legs a big hug. "Don't cry Tom. We all still love you."

Thomas grinned through his tears and leaned down to pick her up. The little one knew just what to say and when to say it. He wished he'd had that gift. "Thank you little doll," he whispered as he hugged her close.

Thomas looked over to where John and Tracy stood holding hands. "I need to thank you two for the outstanding job you did on supplies in East Peoria. I think it's safe to say that we couldn't have made it this far without it.

Tracy pulled John up with her and they came to stand with the small group in front of the fire. Tracy gazed at Thomas fondly. "We all know that you did what you had to do Thomas."

Steven joined them. "That's how it works when we run for supplies. A necessary evil. You've helped me understand that."

Slowly the rest of the group joined Thomas by the fire. All had words of understanding to offer. All assured him that he had done the right thing.

After much hugging and kissing the tired road weary travelers made their way to their tents. They were due for a good night's rest. They had all earned it.

Thomas tucked Emily in with Nancy before

making his way to his own tent.

Josie waited for him. "You didn't have to put yourself through that tonight. We all knew that you did what you felt that you had to do."

Thomas shrugged his shoulders tiredly. "I felt it would be best if everyone knew what had happened."

Josie stood and walked over to hug him tightly. "Thomas we all know what you did was for the best. We never doubted you. You have never let us go hungry and always kept us safe and warm. You always have our best interest at heart."

Thomas hugged her back. "Thanks Josie. That means a lot coming from you."

The two separated and Josie made her way to bed.

Thomas lay down his sleeping bag, pulling his quilt over the top of him. He lay awake for a very long time, remembering the way that it had felt to hold the pillow over Carrie's face.

He had decided that he would go to God by way of the blade. He would never put the group through what Carrie had. He would never do that to Josie.

Chapter Sixteen

Nancy used her free hand to wipe at the sweat that furrowed her brow. She was sweating like a stuck pig. If she had been a smaller girl, like Josie, she was sure she wouldn't sweat as badly.

Nancy turned her face to where Tracy stood with her constant companion, John. It must be really nice to have someone to share everything with. Tracy and John were together all the of the time.

Nancy didn't mind being alone sometimes. But when the nights seemed to be never-ending, and the days were an empty flash of sun, she realized just how lonely she was.

She would like to have someone hold her hand because they wanted to be near her. She wanted someone she could talk to who would really listen and care about what she had to say. She wanted someone to wrap her arms around in the middle of the night when the nightmares wouldn't let her sleep. She wanted her daughter.

She had to be patient, she knew. It was so hard though knowing that Joy was getting closer and closer by the day. Then they would stop and she would go insane inside, not having anyone to talk to about it, not having anyone to share her feelings of dread, of Joy, of sorrow at seeing the child that she could never have.

It was a harsh reality, but a reality, nonetheless. Like the realities she faced each night in her dreams. The reality of abusive parents who didn't want her. Reality of a child she would never know. Reality of a life that would end in one year. With so much unaccomplished in her life.

There were so many realities in her life that there were very little time for anything that resembled pleasure. The only pleasure that Nancy felt from time to time was based on the younger children in the group.

Nancy looked up to discover that she had finally made it to the river. It wasn't really a river, just a small stream.

Despite the cool weather, Nancy took off her shoes and stuck her feet under the sweet blue water. It was really quite a nice day to be out and about.

She was in no hurry. They had decided that it was her turn to fill the water jugs. They didn't need the water until supper time so she had time to daydream.

She could daydream of her daughter. She could daydream of the perfect family that she had prayed to God for. She could dream of a night's sleep without interruption.

She frowned woefully. There was no use in daydreams. She would only awake in terror, remembering her father's words and pawings in the middle of the night, or her mother's screaming that she had not gotten the wax on the floor evenly. She would never feel that she could do anything right.

Her life at home was the cause of the way she was now. She would never be able to be secure in anything. Maybe that was why she was alone. God knew that she could never be secure in a relationship, so he didn't allow her to have one.

The more she thought about it the more she knew that she should never attempt a permanent relationship. Her father had ruined her for all men and her mother had ruined her for all women. After losing Joy, she had a hard time being around some of the children, but she did try harder with them. It seemed in some cases that the child needed her as much as she needed them.

Like Lil' Dawne. Lil' Dawne was so proud and strong willed that it was difficult to imagine her crying or afraid. When they'd found her she was both.

Nancy remembered well the night the pretty little girl had come to be with the group she now called her family.

They had been staying in a park on the outskirts of Miami, Florida when they'd found her.

Thomas had sent Nancy and Wes into the city for supplies during the day. Wes had decided that they would try their luck at picking a few pockets while they were there and headed for the beach. He was sure that they would come along some tourists and get lucky that way.

Well he was right about getting lucky with a few tourists. In fact; they worked their way past a few of the beach bars and got very lucky indeed.

They had headed down to the docks to sit a count their loot and get rid of the now empty wallets when they heard the whimpering cries of Lil' Dawn.

Lil' Dawn had been left by her mother. According to what the little girl told Nancy, her mother had went to score the night before and forgotten her. She had slept under a nearby dock for the night. When she woke, she went to look for her mom, but couldn't find her anywhere.

Wes and Nancy, at the young girls insistence, began to help her search.

They spent the next three days looking for the girls mom, while going back to the camp at night. Thomas was going nuts. He hadn't wanted to stay for long in Miami. He didn't like it there at all.

Nevertheless, stay they did.

On the third night of coming up empty handed. Thomas and Josie enlisted Nancy to coax the story of Lil' Dawne and her mom out of the child.

What they found out made them shudder.

The mother and child were homeless. They stayed in empty warehouses and apartment buildings with other drug users. Lil' Dawne had no idea of who her father might be. She had never met him and really, she admitted, head held high, never thought about him.

The local mission had supplied most of her food, though she was never allowed to go in after reaching the dreaded "school age".

Lil' Dawne was not at all happy at the idea of leaving her mother. She had done nothing wrong, she said adamantly. Her mother needed her to take care of her.

It seemed that when Lil' Dawne's mom got high; she relied on the child for everything. Lil' Dawne took care of getting them food, a place to stay, things to wear. There had been a few times that she had gotten her mother's drugs. Her mother was an addict. If she went without her fix for too long, she would get very, very sick.

The group spent three more nights in Miami, searching for the girl's mother.

They did find her eventually, but they had never told Lil' Dawne.

After asking around, they had discovered that her mother had overdosed and died at a community hospital five nights prior. No one even realized that the child existed.

Chapter Seventeen

Michelle glared at the phone on the end table next to the bed. She was in yet another seedy hotel room. d, deciding to ignore the phone for the next couple of hours. She moved her concentration to the map spread out in front of her on the bed.

She dug through the piles of papers, trying to distinguish what papers went with what case.

She had begun to see a pattern to all to this. She had turned her obsession into a job. About three weeks ago, she had approached a local agency for runaway children in Chicago, wanting to find out more about helping their cause.

She had been invited to attend a fund raising party that same week. She had met and talked with several people about Carrie Dawson and that they were having trouble finding out about her parents.

Seeing her concern and difficulty in these areas, a few of the more influential men and women at the party suggested that she contact them later in the week.

By the time that week was up, they had established her as a child finder. She was now an investigator for the private parties that also provided the backing that she needed.

The pay wasn't all that great, but she loved the work. She had brought herself a little gas efficient Pinto and went out on her new career.

She had, so far, compiled fifteen cases, in the Chicago area alone. She needed to decide what to pursue next. Despite her on-going interest in the Carrie Dawson case, she had other work that she now needed to attend to.

That hadn't stopped her from coming here. She was now in Carrie Dawson's hometown, where she had a meeting scheduled for noon tomorrow with the girls mother. It had taken some doing, but she had managed a visitor's pass to the women's prison where Carrie Dawson's mom was being held.

Michelle had come pretty far in the last three weeks. She had established herself as a child finder and come up with fifteen cases that somewhat resembled Carrie's.

All of these cases had resulted in the death of a sixteen year old where the bodies had been found in a park.

Michelle was convinced that she had found a link. She thought that she was definitely onto something. The thing was that she could not get into some of the information that she needed. The police and coroner's reports were off limits to her.

She kept telling herself that were the only reason that she was considering calling Frank. She needed his badge to get to the information that she could not reach without one.

She knew that this wasn't right. She hadn't talked to him in over three weeks. She had left town without a thought as to how he would react about all that she had done. She didn't want to face him. She had no clue as to what she would tell him.

She knew that he had contacted her father at the forwarding address that she had left at the apartment building. So it was obvious that he wanted to see her. She wondered if it was just for professional purposes or if he really wanted to see her?

She shook her head and glared at the map spread before her. She had to concentrate on her work.

On the map she had marked in bright reds

where the bodies of all the sixteen year olds had been left. She would really like to see the other reports to see if the similarities went beyond the fact that they had all been left in parks.

All of the information that she had so far had been gleaned from the local papers. She had checked all major cities and had come up with fifteen kids. He wondered if the local authorities had established any sort of connection? If they had, there was no mention of it anywhere that she had seen.

That was why she was considering calling Frank. She needed the information that she was sure, with some gentle persuasion, he would be glad to help her out with.

She grimaced and picked up the phone. She dialed the number to his apartment. To her chagrin, there was no answer.

She hesitated before dialing the number to his desk at the police station. She really didn't want to discuss all of this with him at work. She wanted to talk to him as privately as possible.

She frowned and decided that she would go ahead, she would at least leave a message for him to contact her as soon as possible.

Michelle called the police station and

requested his desk. She found that Office Frank Jeffries was not at his desk. She left a message and her phone number at the hotel with the information that she wouldn't be there after ten a.m. tomorrow.

The receptionist said that she wasn't sure when they could get the message to him, but she promised that she would get it to him as soon as she could.

Michelle thanked her and went back to her map. She called the front desk and asked where the nearest fast food place was located. The man said that he was getting ready to send his helper over for their lunch and they would be glad to pick her up something.

She thanked him and had him pick her up a cheeseburger and some fries. She needed the time to work.

She picked through her mess of paperwork and came across a case that interested her more than any. With the exception of Carrie Dawson's.

The name of the boy was Patrick Dempsey. He had been left in a park outside of Reno, Nevada one year ago. Like the others, he was sixteen years old when he died.

The strange thing about this case; was that when he ran away, seven years ago, he took his younger sister Josie with him.

There were reports of abuse in the family, also like the others, but she couldn't see the actual reports without a badge.

She hated to admit it, but she needed Frank. Yes, she wanted to see him for more than just that. She had really liked talking with him and she had a lot that she needed someone to talk to about.

Maybe it wouldn't be so bad. He wouldn't be too angry with her, she hoped. She prayed that he would be proud of her, happy for her new career.

She most certainly was happy with herself. Though in a way, Carrie's passing had been a bad thing. It had certainly changed her life for the better.

She hoped that Frank would understand. She hoped that she would be able to do these children some good. She hoped that Carrie Dawson was looking down on her now and thinking that she was doing the right thing, for all of them.

Chapter Eighteen

Thomas nodded his head at Josie, indicating that they should continue. He wouldn't allow things to get too much more disjointed. They would all have to keep their heads.

Josie grabbed the lead rope to pull Emily's sled and they headed due south. They were preparing to cross the Colorado state line.

Thomas studied Josie's determined face from where he stood under a massive oak tree. If only he could feel that the entire group would be as determined as she was.

The only other one who he need not worry with for the next two hundred miles was Nancy. She knew where they were headed. It was time for their yearly visit to Joy, her daughter.

Thomas shook his head in contemplation. At least they were well provided with supplies.

He had sent Tracy, Steven, and John into a small town called Dodge City when they had left Wichita. They had done phenomenally well there. They had enough supplies to carry them straight through to Golden, where Joy stayed with her adopted parents, Matt and Darby

Golden was only a few miles from where the entire group would stay in Mesa Verde State Park. They would restock on supplies when they headed for Cedar City, Utah.

He cleared his head and joined the back of the group which consisted of Tracy, Steven, and John.

He fell into step with Tracy, who immediately questioned him on where they were to hook up with the next train

He started going over his proposed route, explaining that they would be able to ride for only a short period. There would be no trains to take them where they needed to be.

Tracy nodded her head in mute understanding.

John looked over at him. "Has it been a year already Tom?"

Tom looked at him and grinned. "A year and two weeks to be exact."

Tracy and Steven smiled at one another. Tracy shook her head. "It never dawned on me until now that that's where we are headed. Nancy must be going insane with nerves."

Thomas nodded his head in agreement. "I'm sure that she probably is. It wouldn't hurt if the three of you would use a little extra effort in her direction for the next few days. She could use the added support."

Steven nodded at something in front of him and then pointed with his finger. "What's up with Wes?"

Thomas shook his head that he didn't know. He was certainly surprised to see him stopped. He had Shelley, Kevin and Lil' Dawne with him at one point and now he was on his own with one of the supply sleds.

Thomas broke off from the others and headed to where Wes was stopped.

"What's up?"

Wes gave a nonchalant shrug of his shoulders. "I just need to talk to you about something. Every thing's O.K."

"What did you do with Shelley and Lil' Dawn?"

"I pawned them off on Nancy for awhile. She didn't seem to mind the company."

"No," Thomas agreed, "I'm sure that she doesn't right now. She could probably use the distraction. We're getting awfully close to her daughter."

Wes nodded his head. "I figured that was where we were heading. Incredible isn't it? After all these years, we still manage to get to see her for a bit every year. It's so great that we do this Thomas."

"I don't think, with both Josie and Nancy to contend with, that there would be any other way."

Wes gave a deep chuckle. "Yeah, our women have a way of getting what they need, don't they?"

Thomas grinned. "The thing that you have to remember is that without them we would be without a lot of things. Without them we would be in deep shit."

Wes frowned, letting his eyes move over the ground in front of him. "Come on, we can walk and talk at the same time, God knows we've had plenty of practice at that."

Thomas chuckled again and fell into step along side of Wes. "What's got you so down Wes?"

"Oh, I'm not really down, just overly

concerned, I think."

"About what? We've been doing really well since we broke camp three days ago. We're well set on supplies, all of the children are on good behavior and for a change, everyone seems to be getting plenty of rest."

Wes nodded his agreement. "It's nothing like that Thomas. I'm worried about Josie."

"Josie, what's wrong with Josie? I just talked to her an hour ago and she seems to be fine."

"I'm sure that she is Thomas. I'm worried about her going to this big meeting in Cedar City. It's only a month away. How do you think she's going to handle it all?"

Thomas studied his friends face carefully for a second. "I think, knowing Josie the way that both of us know Josie, that she will do just fine and dandy."

"I know she'll do O.K. Tom, it's just that she's a girl. How do you think that the other heads are going to handle a girl leader? Has it ever been done before?"

Thomas shook his head.   "No, it hasn't. That's beside the point. I'm confident that they will see Josie like we see Josie. She is definitely a strong leader in every aspect of the word. The fact that she is a girl should be the least of their worries, and yours."

Wes thought for a moment before replying. "Don't get me wrong Tom, if anyone knows what a strong and smart person Josie is, it's me. I just worry about how well they will treat her."

"I'm going with her Wes. I know what a group of hellions the rest of the leaders are. I can handle them."

"Why don't you consider letting me come along?"

Thomas shook his head. "Absolutely not. You know that would be breaking the rules. None of the regular chapter members are allowed at the leaders meeting. Under any circumstances. I cannot allow you at that meeting Wes. Don't worry about Josie. She'll be just fine.'

Wes didn't answer, just stared down at the ground that he was covering.

Thomas grabbed his arm and pulled him to a stop. "You do understand that I cannot allow it, don't you Wes?"

Wes didn't respond. He pulled his arm out of

Thomas' grasp and moved off at a quick pace.

Thomas watched him go. He understood how worried he was about Josie. Thomas was worried to. It didn't change the fact that Wes was not allowed at the meeting. He would have to talk to him some more about it. He didn't know what the consequences would be if he did try and go. He certainly didn't want to find out.

Chapter Nineteen

Nancy studied her hands thoughtfully as she made up her pallet. She wondered if her hands were a sign that she'd never be good at anything besides caring for children.

Her hands were fat and puffy. Her fingers short and stubby. She could not play an instrument to save her life. She was not good at writing things down, like Josie. She was not good at figures, like Thomas. She was not adept at stealing, like Tracy, John and Steven. She was not a tracker like Wes. She was only good at one thing, and that was caring for the children.

She smiled at the thought. She was not ashamed of her simplicity, in fact she was very proud of it. It made her useful to the group. It made her stand out as it never had before in her lifetime.

She felt that she was serving a purpose in life. God had meant for her to be here, with these people. It felt good.

Nancy snuggled into her sleeping bag and

tried to find a comfortable position on her pillow. She would have to get some rest today. She was exhausted.

The last few mornings since they had been on the move had been accompanied by extreme nightmares. She had been awakened by them during the day and unable to get back to sleep.

She would have to do better. She was responsible for at least two of the children during the night's walk and they needed her to be on top of things, not groggy.

Nancy lay still for a very long time before sleep would come. When it did, the nightmares came with it.

Nightmares of her daughter Joy in a casket of pure white, laying with her arms crossed at first and then opening as if asking her real life mother to join her for a deep and relaxing sleep.

The faces of Matt and Darby swam across her vision, each puffy and red eyed with tears flowing non-stop. At one point she could hear Darby begging for her daughter back. Then Nancy would scream that she wasn't her daughter and she would run into the arms of her child.

Then she woke up.

Nancy stared stonily off into space for a few moments, wondering if her screams had woken any of the others. She sat up slowly and wiped the sweat and tears from her face.

She looked around slowly and to her surprise found Josie and Thomas kneeling directly behind her.

Josie crawled over to her and pulled her close into her arms "You O.K. sweetheart?"

Nancy began sobbing in response, but nodded her head that she was.

Thomas sat down beside the two young women unsure of what he should say. He watched as Josie rocked Nancy gently back and forth in her lap. Maybe he didn't need to say anything for the moment. Josie was doing what needed doing.

The three sat there for a while until Nancy's sobs lessened.

Nancy pulled out of Josie's arms and studied her two companions. "I'm sorry. I didn't mean to wake anyone up. Is everyone else still asleep?"

Thomas shrugged his shoulders. "It doesn't matter, Nancy, what matters right now is whether or not you are going to be all right."

Nancy stared at him n silence for a minute. "Of course I'll be all right Thomas. I always get a case of the nerves before we go to see Joy. That's all it is."

Josie eyed both of them. "Are you sure that's the extent of it Nancy?" I don't remember you having nightmares like this before."

Nancy nodded her head. "I had dreams before, but they were different."

"In what way were they different?" Josie questioned.

"In my dreams this time, I keep seeing Joy in a casket." Nancy shrugged her shoulders. "I know that Joy isn't in a casket. She's alive and well with Matt and Darby."

Thomas and Josie stared at the girl for a while in open mouth astonishment.

Josie slid back around to where she was facing Nancy. She put her hand affectionately on the girls plump shoulder. "Of course she is Nancy. You are just nervous about going to see her again, that's all."

Nancy nodded her head in agreement. "I'm sure that she's fine. It's just the jitters."

Josie reached for the girl and pulled her tight into her arms. "Every thing's going to be fine."

They sat like that for a while longer before Thomas nudged Josie's arm.

He gestured at the young woman that Josie held protectively in her arms. Nancy had fallen back asleep.

Thomas helped Josie arrange the young woman on her pillow and pulled her blanket and sleeping bag up tight.

He grabbed Josie's arm and pulled her to the side. "Do you think it means anything?"

Josie shook her head sadly. "I don't know Thomas. Who's to say? The only way that we will know is to go and find out. Do you really believe that she would know like that?"

Thomas nodded his head firmly. "Of course I do. I've been around long enough to see a lot of strange things happen."

Josie gestured back towards the sleeping figure of Nancy. "I think I'm going to spend the night next to her, just in case she needs me again."

Thomas smiled. "I think that's a good idea. I'll help you get your things."

Wes watched from under his tree in his sleeping bag as the two rearranged allowing Josie to bed down next to Nancy.

Maybe Thomas was right after all. Nothing to worry about. If Josie could be that strong for Nancy, she should handle the leader's meeting well.

He smiled as he watched Josie cuddle up to Nancy's sleeping bag. He thought of his sister.

He figured he would just as well make sure. At least he would be able to protect this one.

Chapter Twenty

Michelle looked at her watch and then at the phone. He wasn't going to make it again. It was almost noon and she was going to have to fly out of here. She had no choice; she couldn't wait.

She looked around her dismal surroundings for the last time, checking to make sure that she hadn't forgotten anything. She ran over a mental checklist of the things that she had packed in her small case for on the plane.

She was headed for Lockwood, Montana. It was a small city not far from Billings, where her plane would land. It was the hometown of Patrick and Josie Dempsey. The city was not far from an Indian reservation. It made her wonder if they were of Native American heritage.

Well, with any luck, she would find out when she got there.

She let her eyes sweep back across the room. It never hurt to be safe. It would save being sorry later. She had left her toothbrush in Bloomington, Indiana before coming here. She didn't want to have to hunt down a toothbrush at four in the morning again.

She went in to make a final inspection of the bathroom, finding it empty, she grabbed her travel bag off of the bed and headed for the door. With her hand on the doorknob, the phone began to ring.

She frowned at it, trying to decide what she should do. She most certainly didn't want to miss her plane. If it were Frank, she figured she would have a lot of talking to do.

She grabbed it. "Yes?"

"Michelle?" Frank's voice sounded so good over the phone that she almost sighed with relief.

"It's good to hear your voice, Frank."

"Is it Michelle?" He sounded kind of sarcastic.

Michelle let her frown deepen before answering. "Yes Frank. I've missed you terribly. I've been trying to get a hold of you in three cities now."

"I know. I've just missed you every time. I was starting to think that you were doing it intentionally."

Michelle tried to reassure him. "Of course I'm not. Don't be ridiculous. If that were the case, why would I have gotten in touch with you to begin with?"

"I don't know. I was beginning to wonder that myself."

Michelle scowled into the phone. "Can we handle all of this some other time. I have to haul ass out of here or I'm going to miss my plane."

Frank didn't reply, but she could feel the tension on the line increase threefold. She simply didn't have time to deal with this right now.

"Look, I'm headed to Billings, Montana. Is there anyway that you could get a hold of me there?"

"Sure," he responded, sounding enthusiastic for the first time in their conversation.

She quickly gave him the name of her hotel and her room number. After he repeated it back to her, she hung up and headed for the door.

She rushed into the lobby where a clerk pointed outside at the waiting cab.

She thanked him quickly and hurried out to it.

As soon as she climbed in, the driver stepped on the gas. "Don't worry, gorgeous, I'll get you to that plane on time."

Michelle smiled as best as she could manage. "That would be great."

The cabbie eyed her in the rear view mirror. "You married?"

Michelle shook her head no.

"Maybe if you make it back to these parts sometime soon I could take you to dinner."

Michelle shook her head again no.

"What, you got a boyfriend?"

Michelle frowned quizzically for a second. "I'm not sure right now. Can I get back to you on it?"

The cabbie nodded and Michelle sank back into her thoughts. She didn't want to mislead him. She could use all the friends that she could find right now. In her present line of work, you never knew where you were going to be and who could give you vital information.

She wondered what all Frank would have to say when she told him of her ideas. Certainly, he would see what she found out as valuable as she had. She needed more information. It was imperative. He would see that wouldn't he?

On the other hand, the way he had sounded on the phone was anything but reassuring. As far as their personal relationship was concerned, she wasn't yet sure of where it would lead.

She just wasn't comfortable with the idea of taking a risk right now. That's what it would be too, a huge risk. When you became involved with someone you had a responsibility to them. She wasn't sure that now was a good time for her to try and deal with that.

Would he understand her point of view about the entire situation? Surely he would, being a cop and all. He couldn't expect anything serious right now, what with both of their lines of work. He was a cop for God's sake. He couldn't want anything long term to have to deal with either, could he?

Michelle shook her head to clear her thoughts as the cab pulled into the airport.

He pushed away her money and got out of the car. He met her at the trunk and grabbed her two suitcases pulling her along with him.

As they walked on through the airport towards her boarding gate, he smiled at her.

"The least I can do is give you a free ride, since you won't let me take you to dinner." He set her baggage on the belt that would carry it to the cargo hold. "Friends?"

She smiled. "Of course and thanks for understanding."

"Well, don't forget, if you ever change your mind."

Michelle reassured him that she wouldn't and handed the waiting stewardess her ticket.

She turned and waved goodbye to the cabbie. If only everyone she had met in her new career had been as friendly, she would have gotten a lot more of the information that she needed Frank for.

She shook her head and let the stewardess lead her to her seat. She was the last one to board.

She had barely gotten her belt on when the plane began it's approach to the runway.

Michelle stared into the clouds as she dozed off to sleep. She could never stay awake on planes.

Michelle dreamed of Frank, making love to her on the floor of her old apartment. Nope, it just wouldn't work right now, would it?

Chapter Twenty One

Tracy stared up at the clear blue sky as the trio searched the area for a good source of water. Thomas had decided that it would be good for all of them to have a bath before they reached Joy. They would want to be presentable. It never hurt for moral's sake either.

John nudged her, making a grab for her hand. He had been sort of strange lately. Really hanging on her a lot, like he was afraid to let go.

It was all right for him to act that way, but it was beginning to wear on her nerves.

She continued to stare up at the sky, allowing him to take her hand.

He pulled on it, trying to get her attention. Eventually she looked over at him questioningly.

He simply grinned wide. "What are you so spaced off about this morning? You're supposed to be helping me look for water, not staring off at the sky."

Tracy shrugged her shoulders. She wondered

if he would ever really understand her. No, she decided. He was beyond the place that she called her own. He would never comprehend what her life was like, or the things that ran through her head.

She contemplated him silently for a minute until he looked up and saw her staring at him.

"What is going on with you today? You are really starting to worry me."

"Nothing." She shrugged her shoulders again.

John, being the friend that he was, knew that she wanted to be left alone. He frowned at her but remained silent. Her nothings had been increasing lately. He couldn't understand why she wouldn't let him in. They had shared everything for as long as he could remember. What was the difference now?

Tracy watched his thoughts chase each other across his face and began to feel guilty. She knew that this had bothered him, but she didn't know how to explain the way that she'd been feeling.

Tracy returned her gaze to the sky above, letting John's hand guide her through the wooded paths that they now followed. It was beautiful out here.

They had crossed into Colorado a few nights ago, and the scenery had become more and more breathtaking the further they went. Tracy was in love with the woods.

She had grown up in Montana, just outside the Blackfoot Indian Reservation in Browning. She had a wee bit of Indian in her, not enough, she'd always thought.

Maybe that would have made a difference in her life, if she would have had a background to base her life on. Maybe she wouldn't have always felt like an abandoned child, wandering on aimlessly, always alone. Maybe it didn't make a damn bit of difference either way that she went.

No, she didn't consider being alone to be some sort of fatal disease, like the other kids seemed to. Tracy firmly believed that without all of the time that she'd spent alone, she wouldn't be half of the person that she'd grown up to be.

It was a hard life. It didn't matter what path you chose, it would be hard either way.

Tracy had been with the group for about three years now. She had grown to love the people in it and accept their ways as her own. It had made her feel complete, or so she had thought.

Here lately she'd been thinking about her mother and father. As always, she wondered what would have happened had she stayed with her father after her mother had died.

She would never know, she had bailed out before anyone had the chance to question her on the matter.

She wondered what had happened to the others.

Tracy had two sisters and two brothers, all younger than she was. She hadn't seen or heard anything about them since she'd left Montana four years ago.

She had been twelve when she decided to hit the road. After her mother was gone, she decided that she would hate being saddled with the responsibility of four other kids. The responsibility had been hers enough already. Her mother was an alcoholic and died of liver poisoning, so she had an incredible amount of work to do for the other four children, even before the old witch had died. She firmly believed that she would never be able to do anything for them while she was still there, so she had left. At the time, it had seemed like the only logical solution. It had seemed the only way out.

She had no clue as to where her real father was. The man that they called father now was actually the fifth in a long line of men that her mother had married and had children by. She had not seen her real father since she was five. She could barely remember him.

The man that they called dad now was O.K. but he sexually abused her and the other two girls occasionally. Oh, not as bad or as often as some of her mother's other husbands, but enough to make you want to lock your door in the middle of the night. The thing was, you never knew when he might have been drinking and decide to kick it in.

Tracy always thought that if you were an adult male and you wanted something, there wasn't a whole hell of a lot that would stop them.

And so she had left. She had felt; that there was nothing else that she could do to help the others. They would all grow up someday and do as she had, if they had any brains about them.

Her life now was better, she told herself. She didn't have the responsibility of looking after four kids and wondering how she was going to feed them. She didn't have to worry about stealing food from the neighbors, or the local grocery, because her parents had spent the little money they had on booze. She didn't have to wonder if they would get to go to school in the morning, if they all had shoes to wear, or coats in the freezing winter.

Or another of her stepfather coming to see her in the early hours of the morning, making her too sore to function in the morning to get the other kids what they needed for the day.

She simply had to steal.

It all seemed worthwhile. They were on the move constantly, which she loved. They were always together. She never had to do anything that she didn't feel comfortable doing. So she would die in a few more months, but wasn't having peace of mind after twelve long years worth it?

Chapter Twenty Two

John stared at his partners back as she pulled the sled in front of him full of water jugs. She was still lost in space.

He shook his head, completely frustrated by the young woman he'd come to care so much about. Why wouldn't she talk to him? There was nothing that they didn't share.

He sighed with relief as the creek they had discovered on their earlier hike worked it's way into sight. At least this was the final load. They would have all the water they needed for all the baths and the next few days travel. The group would be in great shape.

He didn't mind the work. It made him feel important; necessary to the group. With Tracy and now Steven, they gathered most of the supplies that the group used from town to town.

His was a very important job indeed.

The two pulled the sleds up side by side and began filling the water jugs by submerging them in the crystal clear blue water. They filled the jugs quickly this way and were soon ready to head back to the make shift camp they had set up about two miles away.

Before Tracy had gathered up her last three jugs and turned to put them in the sled, he grabbed for her hand again. "Are you ever going to tell me what's been bothering you?"

Tracy stared at him silently for a few moments. "There are some things about me that I just don't think you would understand."

"I could at least try. Wouldn't you feel better if you talked about it?"

Tracy shook her head negatively. "Not this time. This is stuff that no one ever has to know about me and I prefer to keep them to myself."

John looked taken aback, almost pissed off. He shook his head in disgust and went to pick up the lead roped to his sled.

Tracy hurried over to him and pulled him with her to the edge of the creek. "Look, if you really must know, it's stuff about my past that's driving me crazy. I don't want to talk about it to anybody. It's got nothing at all to do with you."

John stared at her doubtfully. "You know, I think about the past sometimes too Tray, but I never let it get to me like that. There's nothing we can do to change what's happened now anyway, is there?"

"No, you're right about that John. It still doesn't keep it from bothering me. You might say that I have a guilty conscience."

John feigned understanding but Tracy, once again; wondered how well he would understand if only he knew the truth about her secret past. Would he forgive her? Could she ever forgive herself? She felt that she had abandoned her own brothers and sisters only to come and take care of other people's brothers and sisters, while God only knew hat was happening to her own. Could he really comprehend all of that?

John watched her shake her head and gave a disgusted sigh yet again. "You know all about my past Tray. I have plenty to be ashamed of, yet you know every detail."

"Yes, I do. I don't know why John, it's just something that I've never felt comfortable telling anyone."

John nodded and made to get up. There were a ton of things that he hadn't felt comfortable telling her, yet he had shared his most intimate thoughts, feelings, crimes with this girl. And he didn't know a damn thing about her past. He was completely left out in the dark.

John grabbed the leads to his sled and let his thoughts drift back over the things in his past that he should have never shared with anyone. The murder of his own father, and watching his sister die without doing anything to help, allowing his mother to live after all the shit they had to contend with growing up. The beatings, the drugs, the filth.

He should have shot them both. He had more than ample opportunity.

He didn't feel bad about killing his father. He had felt that he was getting even for him taking the life of his only sister. He had watched him beat her to death with a baseball bat, never once stopping, not even after she lay still and silent in death.

John remembered all of the blood that he had to clean up as his mother and father argued over what they should do with the girl's body.

His father finally punched his mother so hard that she had sat down and shut up. He had made John help him gather the little girl and carry her out into the backwoods of Tennessee where she was still buried, to this day.

The only difference was that now, the grave

was marked by a small but beautiful white cross that Thomas and Josie had helped him make and place there a few years ago.

After he had helped his father bury his only sibling, he went to his room and waited. He didn't know what would happen next, but he was not going to be in the direct line of fire.

He didn't have to wait all that long either. His mother had shot up while they buried his sister and now his father was joking her in what he liked to call "Never-never land".

After shooting up, they began to drink and later progressed into the sickening sex acts that only people really stoned could enjoy.

John had sat quietly in his room, waiting for them to pass out. He guessed that the murder would have to be considered premeditated, because he knew exactly what he was going to do.

As the dawn slowly filtered in his tiny, dirty window, the house grew silent.

John carefully ventured out of his room, wearing only his socks.

He spied the two nude forms laying on the living room floor, where not all that long ago, he had mopped up the blood of his now dead sister.

He continued on tiptoe to the room that his parents shared. He went over to the closet and weeded through the dirty clothes and the piles of garbage til he came across what he was searching for. His father's rifle.

He wondered if his dad would be proud of how well he had learned to use it now, if he knew what his son's intentions were.

He pulled his parents bedroom door shut and worked on loading the gun.

After he had it loaded, he crept back into the living room and put the end of the barrel level with his father's head.

He pulled the trigger.

John didn't remember much about it after that. He recalled his mother's screams in a vague, distant sort of way. He had gone into the kitchen and packed a few days worth of food and grabbed what little clothes he had that would keep him warm.

He had walked back through the living room on his way out the front door and stared at his mother, still naked on the floor, covered with his fathers' blood.

He brushed the tears from his eyes as they made the final approach to the camp. He looked over at his still silent best friend.

What could she possibly have to hide that was worse than what he had done? What could she have to shoulder that was more painful then his own crime?

Of course, when they had talked about it Tray had said that she should have done the same thing, had she the sense. Did it make it right?

Chapter Twenty Three

Nancy's growing apprehension was obvious to all of them as they made the final approach to the park where they would be camping while they went in to see her daughter. They made excellent time, but it was still too late at night for them to head into the small town without drawing any unwanted attention. They would have to wait til the morning. It was as simple as that.

Thomas had made a huge point of explaining that to her for the last few hours. He felt badly that they were going to add to her case of jitters by not bing able to go straight into town.

Didn't he think that she still had enough sense left to know that he couldn't risk them out and about. She had been pretty strange the last few days, she would admit, but she hadn't completely lost her mind.

Nancy set the high and mighty Miss Emily down as the group came to a halt in a small clearing in deep woods. It never changed. This was one of the few spots that they felt comfortable staying at over and over again. Nothing had ever bothered them while they were here.

What made it even stranger was the fact that there were two adults that knew of where they were exactly and had been there, but still never bothered them.

The entire group had now come to a complete stop and began to set down whatever baggage they had been responsible for on the walk.

None were really tired, they had made a great deal of the journey on train, so they were plenty rested. They had only had to walk the last forty miles on foot. They had cleared it in about eight days, which was phenomenal, all things considered.

There was some sort of excitement towards the center of the clearing, but it was way too dark for Nancy to make out exactly what was happening.

The next thing she knew, Thomas was standing next to her and grabbing her by the hand.

"Someone's left you a message." He pointed in the direction of the excitement.

She followed him back over towards where most of the group now stood. There, around a huge oak, were a group of bright pink balloons. Tied in the center was a white envelope with her name on it.

Nancy stood in quiet shock for a minute before Thomas nudged her gently.

He grabbed her hand and led her over. "Go ahead. We all want to know what it says, if it's not too personal."

Nancy nodded her head and went over to pull the envelope from the string that held it to the balloons.

She gingerly opened the envelope and pulled out a card. Inside the card were several pictures of the blond, blue eyed child that she had given birth to a little over four years ago.

Wiping at the tears that stung her eyes, she read the words that were carefully hand written on the bottom of the blank card.

It said "Welcome back. We have news for you. Please contact us as soon as you deem possible. Matt and Darby."

Nancy frowned at the message. That was pretty vague, wasn't it? Surely there was nothing wrong. They had never done this sort of thing before though, which did make it odd.

Before she allowed her imagination to run wild on her, she carefully cleared her throat and read the message out loud to everyone.

Thomas and Josie exchanged looks, but other than that, no one seemed to think it the least bit out of place.

They began to pass the pictures of Joy around the entire group, making remarks on how beautiful she had grown.

Nancy sank down beneath the tree with the balloons tied to it.

Thomas and Josie soon joined her one on each side, her constant protectors. "Are you O.K. sweetie?" Josie asked.

"Of course. It just struck me as odd at first. Does it you guys?"

Both simultaneously shook their heads "No".

Nancy shrugged her shoulders. "It's probably just my case of the nerves, creeping up to haunt me again. No big deal, right."

Both again nodded their heads.

"Would you two mind if I camp right here? Under this tree? Can I leave the balloons up til morning?"

"Of course." Thomas agreed with a sigh of relief. He was worried that this would inspire the girl to want to head into town tonight. He wasn't in the mood to have to fight with her and Josie over the matter of safety.

The group slowly handed the pictures back to Nancy and began their separate jobs to get the camp set up for the night.

Nancy rose and joined them. Trying desperately to keep her mind occupied but to no avail. Thoughts of her daughter were everywhere now. It was completely unavoidable.

They weren't all that far from where the child had been born. It was just over the hill to the right.

Nancy settled her sleeping bag and quilt under the tree with the balloons and was preparing to curl up when she looked up into the adoring eyes of Miss Emily.

The little red head girl grabbed her hand. "Will you tell me about the pictures Nancy? Who was that girl? Wes said I was too young to remember."

Nancy shook her head enthusiastically gathering the small child into her sleeping bag.

She went through the pictures, explaining the entire story to the little girl.

Emily fell asleep curled up in her lap. Nancy just sat there with her pictures.

Josie came over and offered to take the sleeping child but Nancy firmly shook her head no.

Josie left the girl but brought her sleeping bag over about ten feet away, just in case.

God it was good to have friends.

Nancy gathered her pictures and curled up next to the sleeping form of Emily.

Maybe the little girl could ward off the nightmares.

Chapter Twenty Four

The nightmares and visions swam endlessly through Nancys' tired mind as she attempted to get some much needed rest.

As she had feared the deep sleep that had alluded her for the past few weeks once again would not come. She tried to stay quiet and still, at least for Emily to get her rest, but to no avail. When sleep finally made it's way to her, it was greeted by the same intense visions that had plagued her for the past few weeks.

At some point in the night, Josie must have moved Emily, for the weight that had once rested protectively against her chest was gone. It had been replaced by the snoring form of Josie, who she was sure had the best of intents, but had left her feeling miserably alone each and every time that she awoke during the restless hours of the night.

When dawn finally came. Nancy was wide awake to greet it. She had not yet gotten up, hoping desperately to grab just a few precious moments of sleep.

Giving up, she went carefully around the still sleeping form of Josie and made her way over the hill, to the spot where she had given birth to her daughter.

She sat down on the ground and cried, good and hard for about a half hour.

When she finally decided that she was ready to face the rest of the group she wiped her face and got up, only to discover Thomas standing silently behind her. She wondered how long that he had been standing there?

She went over to him and he gathered her in his arms, squeezing her tight. "Everything's going to be just fine Nan. Wait and see."

Nancy didn't respond, just cuddled into his arms even further.

"I didn't mean to intrude on your privacy, but I was wondering if you have an idea of who you would like to go with you this morning?"

Nancy pulled out of his arms and stared at him in blank confusion for a second. "Why aren't you and Josie going to come? That's the way that we've always gone before."

Thomas shrugged his shoulders noncommittally. "I just figured you might want someone else to go for a change."

Nancy shook her head. "Oh no Thomas. You and Josie are my very best friends in the world. If there is anything wrong I want you two to be with me when I find out."

Thomas nodded his head is assent. "Well let's get the show on the road then, shall we?"

Nancy nodded, looking fairly enthusiastic, despite her apprehensions.

They headed back for the camp and after a quick breakfast and a round up of the other members, Thomas informed the group of where they were going.

After appointing Wes to be in charge of things while they were gone, the three of them, Nancy, Josie and Thomas headed down the familiar trail along the mountain. They were headed for Joy.

The sleepy town of Golden was just a few short miles from Mesa Verde where the group was camped.

With each mile that they hiked, Nan's jitters reached new heights, heights she never knew existed. She searched her mind, trying to remember if she had ever been this nervous before, knowing that they were headed to see her daughter.

Thomas and Josie kept a comfortable silence, seemingly unaware of their friends new heights of fear.

When they reached the town they skirted it, going all of the way around before actually going in. Matt and Darby lived with Joy at a small ranch style house just across the street with a school. This made it very convenient to wait for the other school children and blend in during the morning rush to school.

They would stay in their little group and nonchalantly watch the house across the street for Matt and Darby to come out with Joy.

The trio waited patiently, finally giving up hope when the bell rang, summoning the other children to their classes.

They eyed one another, wondering what they should do when Nancy spotted Matt's red head sticking out from the door.

"Come on over, you guys. We've been waiting for you."

The threesome once again exchanged looks. They then followed Thomas over to the ranch house that Nancy's daughter called home.

Matt pulled the three of them inside quickly. He gestured to the kitchen that was to the right of the entry way. "Darby's fixing you all some breakfast. It's very good to see you. Did you get our message?"

Nancy nodded her head. "The balloons and pictures were very nice. Thank you."

They all settled down at the kitchen table to stare at Darby's back. She still had said nothing to the visitor's let alone look at them.

The silence was eerie as they all looked at anything but each other, each with their own sense of impending doom.

Nancy, unable to take the silence anymore, spoke up. "Where's Joy?"

Darby slowly turned to face the girl that had given birth to their beloved daughter. She burst into tears. She sank, crying, into the chair next to Nancy's.

Nancy looked back and forth between the two of them, waiting for some sort of explanation.

When none came, Thomas grabbed Darby's shoulder. "What's happened?" We have to know."

Darby started to say something and then shook her head, crying freely again.

Nancy turned to Matt. "Please, what's this all about? I've been having the most horrid nightmares and I'm going crazy wondering. Just tell me."

Matt's eyes watered with on-coming tears. "She's dead."

Everyone's eyes turned to Nancy, who simply bowed her head as if admitting defeat.

"That's what all this has been about, eh? Momma always said that I was physic. That bitch. I'm forever cursed, aren't I?" She turned to face Darby. "Tell me what happened."

Darby rubbed her eyes fiercely to face the cold hard tone of Nancy's voice head on. "Leukemia. She had leukemia. We lost control of her white blood cell count. Just about three weeks ago."

Nancy nodded her head. "When I started having the dreams."

Matt and Darby stared at her questioningly.

Nancy stared in stony silence as the other four hammered out the details of her little girls dying in one of the most fatal, painful diseases that can ever curse children.

Everything faded to black, even when Thomas agreed that they could pay a visit to her grave, she blocked it out. Even when they all trouped out into the garage and the jeep that Matt had offered to take them to the grave in. She would never realize that they put her shocked form in the back seat between Darby and Josie for a reason.

She would not realize anything until she came face to face with the little girls headstone, carved of gray granite. She would not realize that she lay down on the grave and pounded it with her fists, screaming at the injustice of it all. Screaming that God had once again laughed in her face. He had taken the one thing that she had made good, and turned it to dust. He had taken a huge piece of what she considered her only reason to be alive in the first place. He had taken every dream she had ever carried close to her heart and dashed it to shreds.

Her life was over. That was what the dreams had meant. She was not allowed in this cruel, cold, harsh world to be with her daughter. Maybe God would allow her her child in Heaven. But then again maybe not. Who was to say but God Himself.

It was soon time to find out.

Chapter Twenty Five

They didn't make it back to the camp until very late that night. The group was greeted by silence as they approached, only hearing the one long low whistle that gave the all clear from whoever Wes had appointed as lookout for the night.

The camp was mainly sleeping, which Thomas was sure was a good thing, considering Nancy's condition. He didn't want the younger kids to see her until she had gotten herself together somewhat. A lot of the younger kids looked to Nancy for stability. That was something she wouldn't be able to deal with tonight. He hoped that tomorrow would be better for all of them.

They took Nancy to her sleeping bag under the tree, where the balloons still hung, getting her safely into bed.

After settling her down for the night, Josie and Thomas made their way to his tent. They had some talking to do.

As soon as they pulled the flap down, Josie

hugged him close to her. "I still have a hard time believing all of this. It seems like madness."

Thomas nodded his head in agreement. "How do you think that Nancy's going to fare over the next few days?"

"I don't know. I could never picture having to drag her off of that grave today Thomas. I had no idea of what to expect and now with this being the final outcome, I don't know how to handle it."

Thomas nodded his head. "I know. Do you think we should pack up camp and head on for Cedar City?"

Josie nodded her head. "That's probably a good idea. Get her as far away from here as possible for right now."

The two went on making plans for how they would handle the next days events. Josie agreed to sleep right next to Nancy for the next few nights, trying to help the girl through her nightmares.

After the two had agreed on all the other plans, Thomas walked Josie out of the tent and saw her safely settled next to the sleeping form of Nancy.

Nancy waited until she could hear the even breathing of Josie turn into snoring.

She crept out of her sleeping bag and rummaged through her pack for a pen and paper. She took two tallow candles and a kitchen knife and made her way to the spot where her baby was brought into this world.

She couldn't imagine bringing a child into this world just to see it suffer a fatal disease, just to see it ripped away from it's mother by uncontrollable circumstances, just to see it die while she was hundreds of miles away.

She hoped that God was having a good long laugh at her now. Her entire life had been nothing but an endless series of cruel jokes. What was the point of continuing?

She figured if she went now, when her daughter called to her in her dreams, that maybe, just maybe, God would allow her to be a part of the child's days in Heaven.

Nancy sat down in the exact spot that she had brought her Joy to life. She lit her tallow candles and gathered her pen and paper into her lap. She addressed the letter to the whole group. It read as follows:

Forgive me if you think that by doing what I

am about to do is a sin, but I would really like the chance to meet my daughter, get to know my daughter and this is the only way.

It is not that I don't want to be here, with you, all of my friends. It just seems that to me, there is no real need for me to go on living, if I have nothing to live for.

I will always thank you all for everything that's been done for me over these long and lonely years. I will tell God, if I have the chance, what wonderful things that we are trying to accomplish as mere children. I hope that He will understand as I have been made to understand for all of these years.

I will always be here, watching, as I have always been. Take care of the little ones, for they have no idea as to how very cruel that life can be. Give Emily my quilt and Lil' Dawn my sleeping bag. I love you all, Nancy.

Nancy folded the note into a neat square before blowing out the tallow candles and set them on top of it so it wouldn't blow away.

She grappled around a bit, eventually finding the kitchen knife and plunging it into her abdomen.

As she lay quietly, teeth clenched in agony,

hands and body now covered in thick, red blood, a small form appeared out of the woods to her right. She watched as the child came steadily close, hoping beyond all hope that Emily had not been awake to follow her.

The child knelt next to her now dying form and with a strength beyond what four year old should have gathered her into her arms.

"I'm here momma. God said to bring you home now. You are ready. Aren't you?"

Nancy nodded her head painfully as she stared at the little girl.

The blond hair, blue eyed Joy smiled and gestured towards a light that had come to envelope the two. "Follow me momma. We can be together now."

Nancy smiled as the pain faded and gave way to a feeling of intense heat and then weightlessness.

She sat up and gathered her child into her arms. Joy, my only real joy."

The two stood hand in hand, staring at the sky above them until they together picked a star. They began their journey. Both had been alone far long enough.

Chapter Twenty Six

Thomas was wakened to the chill air by the sounds of screaming all around him. He jumped to his feet and ran out of the tent to discover Jose on her knees ten feet from the entrance to his tent, head in her hands, sobbing.

"What in the hell is going on Josie?" He asked as he knelt besides her, gathering her into his arms.

Josie gestured toward the tree where the balloons still were tied, pointing out the fact that Nancy's sleeping bag was empty.

He rocked the girl back and forth in his arms, waiting for her sobs to subside enough to get her to talk to him.

Meanwhile, the others, also awoken by Josie's screams, gathered around the two, all with questioning looks.

Thomas shrugged his shoulders and beckoned to Wes and Tracy. "Will you two please gather the little ones and get breakfast started. I'm not sure about what's going on yet, but from the sounds of things, its not going to be good."

Wes and Tracy nodded understanding and gathering up the little ones, headed for the camps circle.

Josie, finally calming down enough to talk, explained to Thomas that she had woken only to find Nancy gone. She had set off on her own to search for the girl and found her in the birth place. She was dead. With this, Josie burst into a fresh frenzy of tears.

Thomas held her for a few minutes on her and then forced the young woman to her feet. He walked her back in the direction of the birth spot.

Once they had gotten about twenty feet away, he could make out Nancy's still form.

Josie planted her feet firmly and refused to go any further.

Thomas held the girl close to him and then relented, allowing her to stay behind.

He grimaced, attempting to prepare himself for the worst.

As he drew closer to the body, he realized that nothing could have prepared him for what he saw.

Nancy had taken a plain old kitchen knife and ran it clear through her abdomen. There was blood everywhere.

The worst part of it all was the sickeningly sweet smile that adorned the dead girls face. It was if this was the best thing that she'd ever done.

Thomas blinked back tears that were threatening and studied the area carefully. Sure enough, there to the right of the body, were two tallow candle stubs. Jesus, she had taken the time to blow them out, saving them for another use, before she'd run herself through.

He walked over and grabbed the candles, noticing the note that was carefully folded and placed under them. She had probably not wanted it to blow away. Good sweet Nancy, always practical to the very end.

He walked back over to the still sobbing Josie with the note in his hand.

She looked up and quieted. "She left us a note."

Thomas weakly nodded his head.

"Can I see it?"

Thomas pulled the girl down next to him,

where he let the tears run undaunted for a few minutes.

The two clutched at each other, hugging together fiercely. They were afraid to let go.

Thomas finally pushed her away and wiping the tears from his face, opened the note.

He read it slowly and handed it to Josie.

After she'd read it and started with a fresh batch of tears, he pulled her up by the hand. "We've got to get this taken care of quickly and get the hell out of here."

Josie studied him closely. "What are you going to tell the others?"

Thomas bowed his head and pulled her by the hand to get her started heading back to camp. "The truth of course. Some will understand, others wont. We all have to deal with it on our own way."

Josie nodded her head. "What about the note? It's addressed to all of us. That's how we'll handle it. It must be what she wanted."

Josie nodded her head again and the two walked the rest of the way back to camp in silence.

The group gathered around the campfire having breakfast was a quiet one, having noticed that Nancy was no where in sight.

All eyes were on the pair as Thomas made his way to the center of the circle.

He choked through tears explaining the death of Joy and of Nancy. The others all held their emotions to quiet bouts of tears that, for some of them, never seemed to end.

They had some serious work to handle.

The group, all in various sorts of grieving, began to pack their things.

There would be no more said about all of it until they were safe once again. It would have to be dealt with silently for awhile.

Thomas and Wes went to dig a shallow grave and put the still smiling form of Nancy into it.

Thomas stared at Wes, who was the only one of them to still not shed a tear. They continued to work in silence until the job was done.

By the time that they made it back to the camp, everything was packed. They headed for Cedar City.

Chapter Twenty Seven

The group headed at a monstrous pace towards Boulder, where they would take a train in the direction of Cedar City, Utah.

Once on the train there, it would take them practically to the front door of where the yearly meeting would take place.

They were starting a few weeks early, because of Nancy's suicide, but that couldn't be helped. Thomas didn't see to much sense in straying too far off of the beaten path anyway. They would just hang out for a few extra weeks, hopefully getting everyone over the shock of Nancy's death.

Some of them were handling a lot harder than the others. One of the ones that he hadn't expected to have as much trouble with was Josie.

It was proving to be a fatal error in his judgment. Josie was having a hell of a lot of difficulty dealing with Nancy's death. She was blaming herself. She had considered herself to be on watch for just this very thing. How had Nancy managed to sneak past her that night. Her sleeping bag had been but a few feet away.

How had Nancy done a lot of things indeed? Thomas wondered. How had she gotten past Josie? How had she gotten past the night watches that were posted on both sides of the camp? John was on the side that she had to have crossed and swore that he had seen nothing. How had she rummaged through not only her bags but the kitchen supply bags for the things that she had taken with her? How had she not screamed with intense amounts of agony when she'd plunged the knife through her abdomen?

Thomas fought off a shudder at the thought of the dear girl with blood caked on every visible part of her body and her clothing.

Thomas glanced over to where Wes was contentedly chewing on a long piece of grass. Still there had been no tears from this young man. Still there had been no sign at all that any of this had bothered him.

It was indeed different for the rest of the group. They were all silent as they moved through the deep woods at the rapid pace that they had set earlier that morning. That was typical. The part that wasn't typical was the layer of sadness that had worked it's way into everyone, from little Emily to Tracy. If this depressed mood continued for much longer, Thomas had no idea on how well Josie would react to the scrutiny of the other leaders.

Thomas remembered well his first meeting with the leaders and the way that Patrick had prepared him for it. It was awful. He had felt as if he were under a microscope with the entire universe staring at him.

There was no question that he would have to find some way to bring everyone out of this misery. It was his responsibility to see that the entire groups moral once again became a norm.

It was imperative that he get things back to what the group considered normal, no matter how far fetched that seem to be to some people, he would have to find a norm.

His gaze wondered from face to face in the group that he considered his family. How many of the others had the potential to commit suicide like Nancy? Or the potential to run away and go haywire like Carrie had? Who would be next? Would he be able to tell in time? And even if he did, would he be able to stop it?

Thomas decided it would be a good time to talk to Josie about her present attitude. She would be a key player in how the rest of the group would react to his badgering.

Thomas increased his pace to match the young woman's who was pulling the sled occupied by Emily. It had seemed that ever since Nancy's death, the two of them were together. He wondered if that were just one of the minor side effects that would influence the group's entire mood for a very long time. He sincerely hoped not.

"Hey, how's it going?"

Josie looked up with the same agonized scowl that she had worn since discovering Nancy's body at the birth spot. "O.K. I suppose."

"Feel like talking?"

Josie shrugged her shoulders. "About what?"

"How things have gone with this entire group since Nan's death."

Josie turned and looked at him without stopping the sled. "I don't think that any of us are ready to talk about that yet Tom. I certainly am not."

"Oh, I see. You all are just going to stick our heads into your own personal holes of self pity and leave me all alone?"

Josie took her time in replying. "There's no need for you to be acting like that Tom. Of course your not alone in this. We are all together. It's just going to take some time for all of us to adjust."

Thomas nodded his head. "I understand all of that just fine Josie. It doesn't change the fact of the matter that you are going to be responsible for this group's moral as well as where they sleep and what they have to eat and drink for the next few years. You are going to have to help me find some way to boost moral. We have to bring this entire group back to some sort of norm as soon as possible. We are going to have to contend with the yearly meeting in just a few weeks. I want the air cleared long before that."

Josie's eyes filled with tears as she pulled the sled to a stop under a large tree. She grabbed Thomas by his collar and pulled him close. "Don't tell me about my responsibility to this group or to you. You see I've had that test already and I failed miserably."

With this she pushed Thomas firmly away from her and pulled the sled roughly back into the path they had been on.

Thomas shook his head as his eyes once

again filled with tears. He looked after the beautiful girl that he had once been able to get help from with anything.

He had never felt more alone.

Chapter Twenty Eight

Michelle grabbed for the phone and swung the suitcase she was carrying to the floor in one graceful motion. The baggage clerk that had followed her to her room with the other case appreciated the sway of her hips without bothering to hide it.

He would be glad to help her with more than her luggage any time.

Michelle answered the phone. It was Frank. She asked him to give her five minutes and then call back.

He sounded taken aback but quickly agreed.

Michelle turned to the baggage clerk with a stiff smile. She didn't mind him checking her out, but did he have to be so damned obvious about it?

She dug in her purse for a five dollar bill to get rid of him when he told her not to bother. He said that if she needed anything else anything at all he would be glad to help her out.

Michelle gratefully pushed the door closed

after he'd gone out of it and sank down onto the bed. She threw her sunglasses on the table next to the bed and took the barrette out of her hair.

What she needed right now was a nice long hot shower. She would have to wait though. She needed to talk to Frank as soon as she possibly could.

She had studied the cases of Patrick Dempsey and his sister Josie while she was on the plane. There was nothing all that unusual. As a matter of fact, she was beginning to get used to the tales of reported abuse, sexual abuse, drug and alcohol use and repeated beatings that went hand in hand with the new job that she had found. What a life to lead. She shook her hair out and lay back against the bed.

At least there was a good firm mattress underneath her tonight, she thought. The last hotel had been great with that one exception. The mattress had sucked her in. Her back was killing her.

Michelle sat back up and fished a cigarette out of her purse. Frank had definitely been right about that. The more that she was around this kind of thing, the more she smoked. She chuckled to herself. If she didn't die from stress, she would surely die of lung cancer.

The phone rang.

Michelle frowned. So the impatient pain in the ass had decided that he had no desire what so ever to wait the five minutes that she had designated. Typical.

She answered the phone.

Frank had decided right off of the bat that he would do most of the talking. He was going to take a 2 week leave of absence and fly out to her tonight. They needed to talk face to face.

Michelle stared at the phone in open-mouthed astonishment. She had expected to hear a lot of things, but certainly not this. She listened half-heartedly to his continuing banter about how this was the best way that he knew of to handle the situation.

Michelle frowned again. Maybe it wouldn't be a bad thing to see him. It had been a while since she had been laid. She wondered if she should tell him that.

Nah, she decided. She told him that he did not need to worry about getting his own room. He could share hers.

The only response that she got was shocked silence, no argument whatsoever. Good, she thought, I can use the peace and quiet. She got his E.T.A. before hanging up.

It was perfect. She would have plenty of time for a good nap before he got here.

She dialed the number to the front desk, informing them that she would be having company for the next few nights that she was with them.

After taking care of that and grinding her cigarette out into the as tray, she lay back on the bed.

A deep black sleep took her far away to a place that not even dreams can touch.

She awoke several hours later to the sound of the shower. She lay still for a while, feeling out her surroundings. After realizing that it was more than likely Frank in the shower, she rose and stripped down to go and join him.

He held her close under the stream of water and made love to her like never before. He told her that he was in love with her and that she could never leave him again.

She kept patting him. "We'll talk baby, we'll talk." She would do whatever he wanted her to, for now, just as long as the rough hands didn't stop the endless roaming of her body that he so obviously adored. She wondered for a split second if it went further than the touch of the skin.

Frank carried her out of the shower and dried her off inch by inch on the bed, being as tender as a cop could hope to be.

They made love again and again until the wee hours of the morn. She never wanted him to stop. They finally fell into a deep sleep, wrapped together like pretzels until the 9 A.M. wake up call.

Michelle curled back up to Frank. What a wonderful night it had been, but it was the daylight now. Time for reality to shake its weary head and smile hello.

She crawled over the still half asleep form of Frank and fished a cigarette from the crumpled pack on the nightstand. She sat back and lit it asking him if he were awake enough to listen.

After he promised her that he was, she came out with the entire story of her new job and the cases she was working on. She told him outright that she needed his help getting the information that unless she had a badge, were off limits.

She came straight to the point and asked him

if he were going to help her.

Frank didn't respond. He crawled out of bed and popped open a briefcase for a folder which he handed her before climbing back into bed.

She scanned page after page of physical evidence sheets that he had copied.

A tent pole found near where Carrie's body had been found.   Clothing from Patrick Dempsey's body that had been discovered to be sold in the state that they were in right now.

Carrie's home state.

Indiana.

Michelle's mouth dropped open in surprise.

Frank just smiled and pulled her close. "No problem. For you lady, I would do anything."

Chapter 29

Josie crept nearer the sleeping form of Thomas. She wanted so desperately to wake him, to talk to him. But she just couldn't. Not right now, anyway. Maybe later. She would just hope that the time would be right later.

They were on a train headed for Cedar City, Utah. Towards that meeting that she was having the funniest feeling about. If her sixth sense were accurate as it had been in the past then they could expect trouble at the Thanksgiving meeting.

Underneath all of this, Josie had turned into nothing more than a huge quivering mass of nerves. She had never been this scared before in her life. Could she explain that to Thomas in a way that he would understand? Could he ever really understand what she was going through?

She just couldn't face it. After his talk on the way to catch the train, how could she expect him to understand? He had come across as if she were some sort of weakling. Well, she was a lot of things but weak wasn't one of them. And she would be damned if he thought that he could get away with treating her like one. The entire scene was bullshit. How dare he come to her so soon after Nancy's suicide and practically demand that she cheer up. Have to boost morale her ass.

Josie calmed herself and moved to the other side of the freight car where she bedded down next to Emily.

It had seemed that she and the little girl had grown even closer since Nancy's death. They were together constantly. Nothing wrong with that. Josie smiled and laid down next to the sleeping child. She cuddled up to the child for a long time but try as she might sleep would not come.

She gave up finally and went to her back pack to find pencil and a notebook. Once upon a time she had dreamed of being a poet. Once upon a time she would never have thought about being responsible for the death of another child.

Once upon a time she would never have believed that a group like this had ever existed – let alone be a part of it.

Once upon a time indeed.

Josie crumbled the paper and threw it aside in disgust. She just couldn't concentrate on anything. She let her gaze wander through the dark car.

Everyone was asleep with one exception. Wes.

She met his solemn stare across the car and wondered how long he'd been awake. Had he seen her try and go to Thomas just to decide against it?

She hoped not. That was the last thing that the group needed to know. They certainly couldn't have trouble in front of everyone right now. It just wouldn't do.

She raised her hand and waved for him to come and join her. They might as well be together if they were both going to be awake.

Wes made his way slowly towards her, as if not really sure that their talking would be a good thing.

Josie gave him a huge smile of encouragement that seemed to spur him on.

When he finally came to be next to her she reached out and pulled him down so that he were right next to her where she could drape an arm across his shoulders.

Wes stiffened at first but then relaxed against her. If he ever had a friend, she was one of them, most definitely.

"What are you doing awake Wes?"

He shrugged his shoulders evasively. "I just can't sleep sometimes. There are a lot of nights that I stay awake. That's why I'm on watch so much. Thomas knows that I hardly ever sleep."

"Huh." Josie grunted understanding. "I didn't know that you had trouble sleeping. Why though? Do you have bad dreams or something?"

Wes shook his head negatively. "No, guess I just don't need much."

"Huh," Josie grunted again.

They were silent for awhile watching the others sleep.

Wes moved a bit away from her and scooted so that he could look at her face. "You know what I keep thinking Josie? I keep thinking about the look on Thomas face when we were burying Nancy. I've never seen him like that before. I mean, he's always so strong."

Josie nodded her head, thinking that Wes had seen her skirt Thomas a little bit ago. "He's gotta be Wes, he's our leader."

"Yeah, I know. He usually keeps his head pretty well. I just ain't never seen him so close to losing it like I did that day."

Josie simply nodded.

Wes went on. "It must be real hard for you knowing that in just a few months you will be filling his shoes."

Josie remained silent, watching Wes' dark face as he continued.

"Don't worry though Josie. No matter what happens if you need anything, anything at all, I'm the man for the job."

With that Wes reached over and gave her a huge bear hug, the kind of thing that she would never expect him to do. Before she could say a word, the young man was making his way back across the train car.

She watched as he settled himself before smiling and waving good night. She watched for for another few minutes before making her way over to the still sleeping Thomas.

It was time for them to make peace, if he could forgive her for being such a bitch the other day.

She reached out and gently touched his shoulder. "Thomas?"

Thomas looked up at her sleepily. He put his finger to his lips and grabbed her pulling her into his sleeping bag.

He held her close and whispered that everything would be okay.

She snuggled deep into his arms but remained silent.

` He stoked her long hair lovingly until she fell asleep. Everything was going to be okay. He was sure of it now.

Chapter 30

Josie regarded Thomas and Wes with a wry smile. Thank God that the traveling part of this little escapade was over and done with. It was a hard enough thing to have to deal with a huge case of the nerves at having to deal with the meeting of the group leaders, let alone keep everyone happy while they were on the move.

They had reached Cleveland National Forest in the wee hours of the morn last night. They had put off setting up camp until the day had begun. They needed to find a water supply before they set up, they were planning on staying here for awhile, so it was a necessity.

Where they were situated this time had a great deal to do with how and where they set up camp. There were no major cities near-by so they had stopped several times on the way and heavily stocked on other supplies. They were planning on being in the area for at least two weeks. They were almost a full week early for the group meeting.

Josie was thankful in a way, she would have some time to sit and think this way.

She had spent some time talking with both of them about the meeting and the death of Nancy. She was able to let them know what made her feel responsible for Nancy's death.

They, of course, told her that she was crazy for feeling that way. Nancy would have done what Nancy had decided to do one way or another. There was no feasible way the Josie would have stopped her.

Thomas was planning to have a meeting concerning exactly that after they set up base camp. He said that it was high time to clear the air. Nothing more had been said since the morning that it had happened.

Thomas wanted to read that note that she had left out loud to the rest of the group. He thought that it would ease some of the tension that they had traveled with the last few weeks.

Josie agreed that it was a good idea. She hated the still haunted states of the little ones and the depressed expressions of the older kids. It was definitely past high time to clear the air.

Josie got to her feet and began moving about the camp talking softly to the little ones about what they should be doing to help out with getting the camp set up.

Once she reached Emily though, she sat back down and pulled the small red headed child into her lap. She held that child tight in her arms for the a long time, just staring off into space.

Emily allowed Josie her time of cuddling and then grew fidgety.

She turned around in her lap giving her a huge grin. "What's wrong with you? Don't you have tons of stuff to do?"

Josie grinned down at the girl. "You know, I sure do. I just figured that maybe we both could use a hug."

Emily pulled away to stand up. "We can always use a good hug Josie. You always tell me that."

Josie stared after the small child as she stomped off headed for Tracy and John. Josie smiled. They would find something to keep that ornery little girl occupied.

Josie shrugged her shoulders and climbed back to her feet with much effort. She felt so tired. If she could find a quiet spot and lay down she would sleep for hours. But she knew that she could not. Not now at least. She had to help get the camp organized.

Steven, Kevin and Lil' Dawne were back from a scouting expedition to find water. They had found a small creek about half a mile away from the clearing that they were held up in now. They would have to decide whether or not they needed to move closer.

Josie hiked over and listened in on the discussion between Wes and Thomas. Wes was saying that they lacked tree cover and he would think it best to move deeper into the woods.

Thomas was arguing that they need not worry so much here. They would have plenty of watchers posted at all times when the other groups began to arrive.

Josie sided with Wes. Being overly cautious was hardly a crime, she gently prodded Thomas. Wouldn't it better to be safe than sorry?

Thomas gave in under the easy badgering of Wes and Josie with a huge grin. With these two running things, he wouldn't have to be worried about his little group when the time came for him to go to God.

Josie's smiled faded as she realized what he was thinking.

The two of them regarded each other silently as their minds worked together, leaving Wes staring in wonder at the expressions that each of them now wore.

How would they ever manage without Thomas. And just to think that not so many months ago, he and Steven had been discussing whether or not going to God was truly a good thing.

The three broke away from each other, each having their own things to do to prepare camp.

They had decided to move to a small clearing about five hundred yards further into the woods. Steven had spotted it earlier as they had looked for a water source.

Once this had been established, Josie went to gather the smaller children and make sure they had all of their things still put together.

She went to help Darryl find his shoes. He had an obstinate streak in him when it came to wearing his shoes. He was part Indian, he insisted. Indians didn't need shoes.

Josie just laughed and pulled him into her lap to finish tying his high tops.

He complained but allowed her to tie the laces.

Josie went back over to pack up her own

things and turned to find Emily regarding her with a long silent stare. "What's wrong honey?"

"Can I carry Nancy's things this time?"

"Sure you can baby. It's already in the sled that I'm going to pull. How about you ride in the back there with it?"

Emily nodded her red curls and grabbed her pack, waiting to be lifted into the sled.

Once this was accomplished, Josie set off pulling the sled behind her, gathering the rest of her family as she went.

The group sat pace behind her as they headed the short distance to the clearing that Wes had picked out with Steven walking steadily beside her.

Chapter 31

Thomas and Josie settled the camp in long before the noon hour. They had mutually decided that they would have their meeting just after lunch. Maybe if they cleared the air then everyone would be able to get a decent nights sleep.

Josie went to the center of the clearing where they'd already set up a ring of stones to start the fire in for cooking. Once they had a steady flame built up they started lunch.

Josie, with the help of Tracy and Shelley put together a good meal of roast, potatoes and carrots. They'd decided that they would eat a good meal midday and have some sandwiches later.

Wes was busy discussing scout patrols and where they would set up the kitchen supplies for best usage.

Thomas and Steven were with him, listening with growing apprehension to the tension that was apparent in the young man's voice and actions.

The three were close friends, but there were just certain things that you didn't discuss with Wes and this was one of them.

Josie had already begun fixing plates for the little ones when the threesome came over for their meal.

The conversation around the campfire during lunch was limited as if everyone knew that something was wrong.

After the group had finished and cleaned up Thomas went to stand where the campfire still blazed. It made an interesting back round for what he had to say.

He began straight away with reading the note that Nancy had left when she died.

Many of the small group cried when he'd finished. Others sought the comfort of whoever had the closest arms.

Thomas gave everyone a few minutes to gather themselves together and then went into a lecture about the morale of the group and how they would have to find a way to improve it in leaps and bounds over the next few days.

He would like to see a lot of happy, smiling

faces, not just for his benefit, but for the benefit of Josie.

He went on to single her out, saying that she would need a bunch of hugs and kisses. She would need everyone to be smiling and happy for she was about to go through the initiation process with the other leaders.

He began to discuss how many other groups there were and what sort of information they would pass around at the meeting that was only a week away.

He wanted the rest of the group to keep this in mind as they were each given more of the chores that were usually his and Josie's. They would have to arrange the cooking and the watch schedules so that he and Josie would be free to attend all of the meeting. They would have to be responsible for the smaller children more than they usually were.

He finished by reminding everyone that though this week would be stressful for all of them, that they should keep their chins up and remember in a few weeks it would all be over.

Emily, feeling dismissed, came over to crawl into Josie's lap. "You know I'll be good, don't you Josie?"

"Of course you will sweetheart. I think Thomas was just reminding us all that we should try and be as good as possible also."

"Oh." Mumbled Emily as she gave her a brief hug. She rubbed her eyes sleepily. It was time for the child's nap. "Will you come sleep with me for awhile Josie?"

Josie nodded her head in agreement and they headed for Thomas' tent. It would be the only quiet spot in the camp until nightfall. There were still many things that needed to be done, but Josie was in dire need of some sleep.

She didn't think that the others would mind if she napped for awhile.

Josie curled up with Emily in Thomas' sleeping bag.

Emily mumbled sleepily til she dozed off. Once she had a full belly and was warm, the little girl could sleep almost anywhere.

It reminded Josie of how they had found her.

The group had been camped in Crescent Beach, just outside of Portland, Maine, when they'd found the baby.

Someone had left the child in a trash can in the park where they had begun to set up camp.

She had been cold and hungry, screaming at the top of her lungs.

It was odd, now that she thought of it, for the two who had discovered her had been Carrie and Nancy, both who were dead now. The two had been scouting for a water supply when they'd heard the babe's tired cries.

They had brought her straight back and between the three of them, they had nursed the child back to health in a few weeks. It had been no small feat either. For a group on the road, they had none of the necessities for taking proper care of an infant.

They had sent John and Tracy in to Portland with a list of needs a mile long. And as always the terrible twosome came through with a bang.

By the time they had returned, they were laden with diapers, bottles, formula, even some baby clothes.

They were set.

Wes and Steven returned to the trash can that they'd found her in and took turns watching for the next few days. They thought that maybe the mother of the child, or whoever had put her there, would return looking for her.

They had been surprised to see a young man approach the can on the second day.

Wes followed the young man back to a seedy motel and waited while Steven doubled back and talked the matter over with Patrick and Thomas.

The three decided that it would be best for the child to remain with them, regardless of whether they had found the parents or not. If the conditions that Steven had described having followed the young man back to, then they would raise the child as best they could with the group. The parents had obviously not wanted her in the first place if they had left her in a trash can, regardless of the circumstances.

They had decided that it was to be, and while Steven went after Wes, Thomas and Patrick held meeting and told the rest of the group of their decision and why.

Patrick walked over and fondled the head of the child lovingly. Josie remembered it so well.

It had been just a few months before Patrick had gone to God.

Josie hoped to be half of the leader that her brother had been. He was so certain of all of his decisions, so confident.

Josie snuggled the youngster closer under the sleeping bag. She would do whatever she had to keeping these precious ones safe and warm and well fed. Whatever she had to.

She fell asleep, dreaming of her brother and of Wes.

Chapter Thirty-Two

Michelle rolled over in the bed and rubbed her eyes. On the pillow next to her was a note from Frank, saying that he had gone to scrounge up some breakfast and the morning papers.

Fine with her. She rolled back over and pulled the pillow tight over her head. She felt as if she could sleep for a few days straight.

She tried to doze off but found that she couldn't. Even though her body was in need of rest, her mind was running in dizzying circles.

She still did not know anymore on where she stood in her relationship with Frank than she did when he arrived here three days ago. Sure they had great sex and they were compatible, but was that enough to base taking such a huge risk on?

She still wasn't clear on it. It was going to take some time and some serious consideration, Frank had reassured her. He was willing to wait as long as she needed him to.

Pretty damned considerate of him, wasn't it?

She tossed the pillow aside and sat up, grabbing for her cigarettes.

She had just lit it when she heard the key in the door.

Frank let his grin spread across his face as he entered the room with his arms full of newspapers and a bag of groceries.

"I should have never gone shopping while I was this hungry. You wouldn't believe all of the junk food I brought."

Michelle laughed. "Of course I would Frank. You cops have a junk food and donut fetish, don't you?"

Frank shrugged his shoulders and grinned sheepishly. "I suppose we have made a name for ourselves in that department, haven't we."

Michelle climbed out of bed and helped him with his purchases. "Did you buy anything that I might want to eat?"

He laughed at her and tousled her already angry mass of hair. "Why don't you look while I go and get your hair brush. You're going to need help getting through that mess."

Michelle picked through the bags that he'd bought, setting aside a box of donuts, a package of sweet rolls, and a box of pop tarts. She finally coming across a bag of apples, and a bunch of bananas. He had thought of her.

She sat down in the chair and peeled a banana while he began brushing through her tangles.

She pulled a copy of one of the newspapers that he'd brought back and glanced through it, stopping time to time on various articles.

Frank glanced at that she was reading from time to time over her shoulder, not really paying attention. He was busy trying not to tear any major amounts of hair out of her head when she grabbed his arm and pulled him down into the chair next to her.

She shoved the paper that she'd been holding into his face.

The top of the article read. "Bloody Suicide of Sixteen Year Old Being Investigated."

Frank went on to read about the girl and how she had taken a plain kitchen knife and ripped her guts out in the middle of the park.

Frank set the paper down in a state of shock. It was either a major breakthrough or a bizarre coincidence.

He looked over at Michelle, who sat crying, staring stonily off into space.

He knelt down in front of her chair and pulled her into his arms. "How do you want to handle this?"

Michelle shook her head and wiped her eyes. "I want you to get on the phone and get us the first plane out."

"Don't you think that you're jumping the gun a bit?"

Michelle shook her head no.

Frank stared at her for a second. "Well I think we should take our time. We still have a ton of work to do right here."

Michelle stared at him as if stunned. "You don't even realize, do you?"

Frank stood up and began pacing. "Realize what? What is there that I'm missing in all of this? I know how upsetting it is to hear of another dead child Michelle, but, I'm telling you in your new line of work, you'd better get used to it."

Michelle stood up, pushing her chair hard away from the table. "Nancy Leads, the girl that committed suicide, is one of my cases."

Frank stopped pacing and watched her as she made her way to the bedside phone.

Michelle dialed the airport and asked for the first flight out, before she ordered the seats, she asked him if he were going.

He merely nodded. Of course he was. He would never be able to forgive himself if he didn't.

After she had made all of the necessary calls she headed into the bathroom.

She poked her head outside of the door before climbing into the shower. "By the way Frank, I'll never get used to it. A child dying in the middle of the park is something that no one should ever get used to."

Chapter Thirty-Three

As Michelle and Frank boarded their plane headed for the mountains of Colorado, the group settled in for a good night's rest. They had all decided that since they had settled themselves so early, that Tracy, John and Steven would begin a supply hike into the nearest city at dawn.

Thomas wanted to be sure that they were adequately supplied with all of the necessities before the meeting started. He wanted everything to be as worry free as possible for Josie and the rest of the group. There would be enough things for them to worry about over the next few weeks.

The suicide of Nancy had not been brought up again. After Thomas had made his speech on the day of their arrival, they had come to terms with her death, at least most of them had.

They all learned that there would be changes that they would have to make and learn to live with, from the oldest to the youngest. It seemed that regardless of your age or station in life, there were always things that had to be dealt with, one way or another.

Darryl had learned the hard way that changes were always coming. Even at the strangest times, things could get completely out of control.

The theory behind the group was perfectly clear to young Darryl. He even agreed with most aspects of the rules that they were to follow.

The thing was, that even though he knew that the rules were beneficial to the safety of all of them, he still had a hard time accepting some of them.

Rules were something that Darryl had problems with before. When he had lived with his parents, the entire house had seemed to be one big rule, with no gray areas in between.

As a child growing up under the strict rules of a preacher and his wife, Darryl soon learned that there were ways to get around the rules. Most of them anyway. In his short life he had quickly advanced over the stages of maturity that most of the others had years to deal with, to adjust to. He never had.

He remembered what had happened the day he'd left his parents. He remembered how deeply shattered he had been inside when he'd seen his father on the sofa of his church office with a very young girl.

He decided that there were no rules worth playing that would amount to this. He decided that though his father was sworn a die hard servant of God he had still found a way to break the rules. So why should he have to deal with rules from someone who so quickly became a hypocrite.

When he'd spent the better part of the evening trying to come up with some sort of valid reason to help him to deal with the situation he experienced the second shock that sent him packing.

He realized from listening in on his parents late night conversations that his mother was well aware of his father's sexual habits. Not only was his father a hypocrite, his mother condoned his actions by being a hypocrite herself.

Darryl packed his things and set out in search of something different. Not better, just different. He wanted to taste the reality that he felt he had missed in all the years that he'd spent living with the hypocrites.

He'd met Shelley in the back woods of North Dakota. It had been the beginning of the fall and he was trying to decide the best way to handle the winter on his own. Shelley had come across his camp site in the middle of the night and woke him. She had told him that there were dogs out in the area in search of a runaway boy.

He never admitted to her that he was the runaway that the authorities were looking for. He simply told her that he was in need of some help. He needed to be hidden until the authorities cooled out with the search parties.

He told her that he did not want to be discovered under any circumstances.

Shelley took him to Thomas.

They had been camped about twenty minutes from him when Wes sounded the alarm from the camp to make a hasty retreat.

Many of them had simply hid their things the best that they could and headed for the trees. The others had decided that they would seek out the cause of the alarm.

Shelley had opted to find the cause of the uproar and discovered the young man, He'd had no shoes on and his dark hair and eyes made her think of an Indian.

Darryl never discussed his back round with the others. He simply told Thomas that his parents were hypocrites and that he didn't think that he could ever look either of them in the face again.

Thomas accepted the explanation with a shrug of his shoulders. He figured that if given time, the boy would come around to someone in the group.

It never happened. After they had made their escape and crossed the state line to South Carolina, they were no closer in their knowledge of Darryl than they had been when Shelley had found him.

Thomas continued to be patient. There were others in the group that had not been so straight forward in their telling of where they were from and why they were here.

Thomas felt that he should not have to ask, but once the rules of the group were explained and the option of joining were given, everyone should be welcome with open arms.

If you told someone that they were only allowed to live until the age of sixteen and they still wanted to join, that was sufficient evidence to Thomas that they needed to be with them instead of whatever type of nightmare past they had left.

That was perfectly alright with Darryl. He felt that he didn't have an abusive enough life to be with these children. He felt that he were the outsider looking in.

Sure, he had bonded with some of them. But they still considered him too young to be given certain responsibilities and too old to be babied.

He wondered once again as he stared into the inky black of the night sky through the treetops, if he should go to Thomas with his visions.

He didn't want to be laughed at. He had always hated that. He would rather keep his dreams to himself than risk any sort of humiliation.

This decided, he pulled his sleeping bag tight over his head and opened his mind to the clouds.

The clouds that would take him beyond this patch of forest, past this night, into a place where the blood and screams of his new family were filling the air.

CHAPTER 34

Thomas and Josie curled up against a box of toilet paper in his tent going over the maps of where they had been this past year. It would be gone over at the meeting where the group had moved through. Once it was recorded with the other groups they tended to avoid the paths that were heavily tread.

They had gone over what her part would be in the meeting and the testing of her knowledge as to how the group managed to get along. She would be studied intensely.

Josie tried not to let it bother her and thought back to the stories that her brother Patrick had told her about meetings he had attended as leader. Different groups were handled in different ways. There were no set guidelines on how to proceed. The rules were few and simple. No one told them how to exist, survive.

They were Violators. They managed on their own.

Thomas studied the pretty young girl thoughtfully for a moment as she studied the map on the ground in front of her. There was no way that the other leaders would not see the perfect love in this girl. There was no way that they would not see that she was the obvious best choice. Thomas hadn't had to consider who would replace him for more than a second.

Josie was perfect. Her brother had taught her well for almost five years before going to God. With Patrick as her brother and mentor, there was no getting around Josie being left in charge of the group for the next three years.

She looked up at his silence and caught the cautious smile turning up the corner of his mouth. "What are you smiling about?"

The grin went full fledged. "About picking the best possible leader this group has ever seen."

She grinned back. "I am nervous and trying not to show it. I don't want Emily or Lil' Dawne thinking I am scared." She shrugged both shoulders and looked down. "But I am. I am really glad that we will be together."

Thomas lowered himself to sit across from her. "Nothing to worry about. Yes, we will be together the whole time. I promise."

Josie grimaced once more and shrugged her shoulders. "I remember Patrick saying once that there were different kinds of people for different kinds of things. He said that God would let us know when things were right. Just knowing what kind of brother I had in Patrick makes a lot of difference in me being who I am. I am ready to be the leader of this group." She shrugged again. "I am sure on that."

Thomas nodded his head thoughtfully and turned her attention back toward the map. "You should stick with Texas and New Mexico for awhile. We haven't been through there in almost five years."

Josie laughed. "You have a sight for the map Thomas. I have a sight for the kids. The mapping you will have to get me used to."

They ducked their heads together again over the maps that would take them across the country – park by park.

CHAPTER 35

The other groups began trickling in the next day, making the flurry of activity a crazy happiness at being together in a large group for a change. Different people would amble by and exchange "Hello's".

Three people were nominated each day to help with preparations for the meeting camp fire circle. Thomas sent Wes with John and Steven for the first day. There was a lot of heavy lifting to do.

They gathered stones for the fire circle and drug felled logs for seating. One of the gathering groups had come across some hay bales and they were setting these about in different spots.

There were to be sixteen people present for the meeting this year. Thirteen leaders and three leaders in training all arranged around the camp fire.

The group split up to scout for felled burning timbers, John being with Wes.

Wes had been unusually quiet today, but John bugged it off as due to the strangers. He waited until they were well out of ear shot before prodding the young man. "What's up with you today

Wes? Been awfully quiet."

Wes shook his head at his friend and smiled. It was a typical response.

John decided on another approach. "Out here gathering up all this fire wood for a fire we ain't even allowed at! Some meeting!"

Wes stopped and stared at the ground for a second. "Maybe one of us should be there. Just in case. Josie's first time. Ya know?"

John stared at his young friend in astonishment. "Thomas will be right there with her Wes. There is nothing to worry about. Josie will be fine."

"Uhmm." Wes replied as he hurried to move over to another piece of tree.

John went on to warn his friend. "We aren't supposed to be anywhere near the meeting Wes. No matter how you feel about it, we just can't be here."

Wes just shrugged his shoulders and went out of hearing range from John.

John toyed with the idea of mentioning the odd conversation to Thomas when they returned. No need to upset the balance of things. He just hoped and prayed that Wes would listen.

Wes had a keen sense of things though. If he sensed there were a need for him to be close to Josie, he would see it through.   He and John were both protective of the girl who would soon be their leader. And after the crazy deaths of both Carrie and Nancy they would need to be on their toes. Just in case.

Chapter 36

Michelle dropped into the back seat of the investigators cruiser, exhausted after the long seven hour trip to Denver. The drive through the mountains was glorious as November hung on with beautiful colors for the ride. Such a gorgeous setting.

She and Frank had no sooner stepped off of the plane to be met be a fellow police woman, named Maranda. Frank had worked over time on the phone in locating and explaining the situation to the cop.

Maranda was game for any help she might get, as there were no leads, no forensic evidence, nothing. There was no need in such a clear case of suicide, but she had a lot of questions. Like who buried her after she'd done the deed? She met them at them at the airport to escort them to the site of Nancy Leads death.

On the drive through the mountains to the state park outside of Golden, Maranda asked her about her interest in the case.

"Just trying to figure out why all of these kids

are running around in the woods, no parents, friends, family. There is a lot of abuse going on out there and no one is really doing anything about stopping it. We are just dealing with the end result. Trying to figure out the why's. What sad shape we are in."

"Trust God to know the right in all things. That's how I sleep at night. And more power to you. Maybe if more of the facts of these things are brought to light, we can better deal with them in an effective way. But right now, you are right. There just isn't enough being done." Maranda reached over and patted her on the shoulder. "We need a bunch of people with good souls like you."

Maranda handed her the case file to look over, which she passed to Frank in the front seat. They continued the drive up the mountain in silence. They were soon shrouded by huge trees and turned to the east on an old logging road. They were out in the woods some distance.

After another fifteen minutes, Maranda pulled the vehicle to the shoulder of the road. "Have to hoof it from here." She looked down at Michelle's sensible hiking boots and grinned. "Sure good to meet another bright and beautiful woman investigator."

"Frank made sure we both had a pair." Michelle smiled indulgently at her partner.

They trudged on for about a mile and a half before veering to the left. There, in a small clearing, was an area taped off with yellow police tape.

Besides the blood on the ground, there was very little in the way of seeing. But there was a feeling to the place. A peaceful acceptance.

"Not much to see here. She was buried about four feet deep. A bit complex for a suicide. Unless someone found her before us and tried to cover her up?   But the truly curious part is just a bit further."   There she stopped and pointed. There was more police tape around a huge oak in the center of a gigantic clearing. There was a fire pit set with logs pulled around the outside to sit. There was a water pump on a cedar chip trail about a hundred yards out of the wood line.

"Home sweet home." Frank mumbled as he and Michelle headed for the tree.

There were two pieces of balloon string clipped short to the tree.

Chapter 37

Wes repositioned himself to better study the faces of the leaders carefully. There were a couple that made him wonder? Corey especially had his attention.

Before Thomas had introduced Josie as the incoming leader for the group Corey sullenly stalked through the camp fire pit with a slightly smaller boy to glare at Josie. From his position in the tree he could not make out the details of Josie's face but he could sense her uneasiness as surely as he could see Corey's hostility.

The group leader, a guy named Drew, who was also appointing an incoming leader, was doing his best to keep a lid on the situation. It was proving difficult with Corey.

Each of the leaders were given a chance to ask the appointed heads three questions.

Josie had been the first of the incoming leaders to be questioned and she was stuck with Corey playing on the hard ships of being a girl. It was more than Wes could bear.

He had stationed himself in the same spot for

the last three days of meetings waiting for this. He was sure that it would not end well.

There was a shutter in the tree behind him. He was suddenly headed for the ground with an arm wrapped around his waist.

Corey was the first to approach. "What is this? We have us a spy!"

Wes found Josie's wide opened horrified eyes at the same time Thomas pushed through the crowd.

"What are you doing here Wes?"

"Just checking on Josie." Wes shrugged, lowering his eyes from Thomas'.

Corey clucked his tongue. "Thats too bad, Wes, is it? Looks like you may have heard too much. You will go to God."

Drew knelt down to Wes. "Moving a bit quickly on that don't you think Corey? Let's see what he's heard."

Thomas instantly came to Wes' defense. "I am sure that whatever was heard can be trusted with this young man. He was Patrick's 2nd and my 3rd. He was simply concerned with Josie becoming the first girl leader. He was taking care of his friend."

Corey gritted his teeth. "There is no matter of friendship at stake Thomas. It is simply unheard of to be caught spying on a yearly meeting. He needs to be confined and questioned by all of us, to see if we have been jeopardized."

Thomas shook his head. "There is no need for that. We will take him with us to our circle. You may question him in the morning."

"Drew? There is no need to treat him as anything but weak minded. He is no spy. I stake my life on it."

Drew shook his head. "Sorry Thomas. He should be locked up or kept under third party guard until we have a chance to question him."

Thomas got to his feet. "Please, just let us go home. You can keep me instead."

Corey leaped up with his hands on his hips. 'So that you can instruct him further Thomas? I really do intend on figuring out what it is that is going on here. You should be locked up as well!"

Josie's jaw dropped open as she watched as Wes and Thomas were herded into cages and left near the bon-fire. Every move that she made toward them was blocked.

Chapter Thirty-Eight

Josie cried so hard that she was shaking as she walked. The first bush that she came to stand near she crushed in her hands to try and steady the shaking.

As soon as she could control her movements she headed for Tracy and John. They would need to be in on this. This was a set-up. This was not right. They were just looking for a reason to start trouble with their group, and they had found it. They didn't even have to center on Josie's being a girl. Wes had provided them with an excuse. Josie didn't know why. But she knew that she was right.

She went straight into Tracy and John tent. After telling them what had happened at the meeting they had agreed with her. John volunteered Steven to go and help Josie rescue the Wes and Thomas. John and Tracy would wake the others and get them on their way.

They knew that the key to moving successfully at this point was their timing.

It was then that they heard the shots. Two of

them timed about fifteen seconds apart.

The three of them stared at each other in shocked silence as the reality of what they had just heard sunk in.

Then they were moving.

Josie grabbed Steven from his sleeping position against a tree and raced back toward the bonfire for the meeting. Slowing down and keeping to the trees the closer they drew, they could make out five figures gathered around the two lifeless bodies in the center.

Josie grabbed Steven and spun around but it was too late. They had been spotted.

"We won't hurt you. We just want to talk. Absorb what is left of your group into ours. No girl can run one of these groups! Girls just don't have the balls!" Corey chortled.

Steven was well out ahead of Josie when she heard the next shot ring out.

Josie could barely restrain her cry as she doubled back to her left.

Steven was dead.

Thomas was dead.

Wes was dead.

There was nothing left to do but run.

Chapter Thirty-Nine

And run they did.

Chaos erupted as Josie was making her way clear of the shooters and the shootings. She could hear the screams of the other leaders as they tried to understand what had happened. No matter. None of hers would be sticking around to find out.

John and Tracy had been instructed to grab the kids and what they could carry and head for the train.

They headed back to the tracks and out of the park in record time. They were headed south to south east – hopefully crossing the New Mexico border soon.

What remained of their group was a sad little bit of a memory of what was at the last full moon, Josie wiped the silent tears from her face and wondered what she could do now? How could she protect all of these innocent babes?

How would she manage to keep them out of the range of those insane people back there?

How would she manage without Thomas? Or Wes? Or Steven?

The three had quickly and thoughtlessly been taken from her at the worst possible time! How was she to survive and provide for the others with so many key pieces missing?

They rode the train through the night and into an over cast morning across the New Mexico plains.

Most of the group had eventually gotten comfortable and passed out for the ride.

One of the exceptions was Darryl. He woke at about three in the morning and came to sit next to Josie, who was staring out of the slightly open door at the plains as they rolled by. She was crying but it seemed as if she were always crying these days.

Darryl sat quietly and only took her hand after a few moments.

They stared out the door together for another hour before Darryl reached up to wipe the tears from Josie's face.

She looked at him for a long time, not saying anything. Then she reached over and hugged him with all she had.

It was an intense hug. One that lasted for awhile. One that really meant something. One that would heal her soul.

"What would I do without you Darryl?" She finally sat back and examined him for a moment. "What do you think of this mess?"

Darryl looked at her for a minute and then turned his attention back towards the door. "Josie, I've been having some really strange dreams lately. About all of us. Just doesn't make any sense, they keep changing too. I don't know. I am worried about what happens next."

Josie gave him a wistful smile. "Don't sweat it big man." She reached out and gave him another brief hug. "I've got this."

With this Josie hopped up and headed for where John and Tracy were curled up with Emily. She woke John up and explained where they were. She instructed him to wake her in three hours.

They would disembark somewhere in Texas, near the White Bayou Reservation. It would be a good place to lay low for awhile til she could get a grip on things.

Chapter Forty

Josie snapped her head up at the sound of leaves crunching underfoot just about fifty yards from her perch in a tree.

She was right.

They were being followed.

Just how that had come about she had no idea. How they had figured out where the train they were on was headed? How they had figured out where they had gotten off?

They were all going to be shot. No doubt about it. She would not have the strength to keep running for any longer.

It had been ten long days on the run now with no specific breaks. They had moved by foot from the tracks down south towards a camp site they had stayed at years ago.

She trained her eyes in the direction of the leaves crunching under foot. It was a doe. A beautiful baby doe. She was fawn color coming so close that Josie could have leaped from the tree to her back.

Suddenly, the deer froze and looked in Josie's direction.

Josie stared back.

The doe sped away quickly leaving Josie to sit and stare in shock at what had just happened.

At least it wasn't Corey.

John had reported seeing Corey on a scout run just three days ago.

That had been the last time any of them had sat still until today. It was only Emily crying from exhaustion that had given Josie the incentive to stop for awhile and let the group eat a decent meal, though she would not allow a fire.

She was on watch for this side of the make shift camp and Tracy was at the other. She was not comfortable sitting still any longer than three hours.

They had to keep moving.

Unless... she reached down into her back pack to stroke the pearl handled .22 tucked in with it's box of bullets. She'd always known that Thomas had it.

The gun had been Patrick's before he had passed it on to Thomas. The gun was for emergency purposes only. It didn't get to be more of an emergency than right now.

Josie moved her hands through her hair. She was pulling it out from fretting with it so much. The mouse brown curls clung to her fingers in unwashed oiliness. For the days when they had the luxury of bathing!

They simply could not go on like this.

She had to make a choice and make it count.

They could not go back to society.

They would be placed in foster cares or orphanages until they reached eighteen years of age unless they were returned to their families.

Josie shook her head at this thought and rubbed her temples in small circles to relieve the head ache pressure.

She could walk away with the little ones and leave John and Tracy with Shelley.

How she would manage then God knew.

She could take the gun and end it now. Send them to God now, where they would be safe and loved and well cared for.

What other option did she have?

Send them back to the families that had put them here or worse yet in foster care in uncertain families to deal with more abuse?

Let their pursuers catch up and finish the job in destroying Josie's happy little family?

Keep running?

She could not run anymore.

Chapter Forty-One

She took them one by one into different parts of the bayou.

She started with Tracy and then John. Shelley and Lil' Dawne and Darryl. She took them into the edge of the water of the White Bayou and ended the lives of her family. She did it with complete love in doing what had to be done. She would not let them suffer anymore. Not by society's hands. Not by the hands of the others like them.

She did it.

When she put the gun to the back of Emily's head and pulled the trigger she lost it.

She sat wearily on the bank and considered what to do next. She should end her life right here right now. But she couldn't. She just didn't have the strength.

How long she sat there she didn't know.

It was hours or maybe days. She was cold and wet, filthy with mud and blood of her brothers and sisters.

Josie got to her feet put the gun back into her back pack.

Chapter Forty-Two

It was a miracle that she found them. They were hiking around the site of Thomas and Wes' bodies when she returned there.

She still hadn't bathed.

She hadn't eaten.

She was exhausted.

Michelle and Frank put her in the back seat of their rental car and took her to a motel.

She bathed. She ate. She slept.

For three days the young girl slept with Frank and Michelle taking turns keeping an eye on her.

They were the only ones who knew of her existence.

When Frank saw the news reporting the three murdered boys in Cleveland National Forest he and Michelle hurriedly packed their things from their stay in Colorado, thanked their new found friend Maranda and headed for the park.

The bodies had been cleared off before they

had arrived. But much remained.

There were tents and camping gear. Personal items and clothing, food and drinking supplies. It looked to have been cleared in a hurry. What a mess to leave behind for processing. It would take the Colorado State Police months to sort out the evidence.

Michelle and Frank had been hiking the outer perimeter when they had spotted Josie.

They had decided to smuggle her out and keep her to themselves until they had some answers.

Who was she and what part did she play in the deaths of those three boys?

None of which were cases Michelle had ever heard about.

It didn't matter. She was sure that the girl in the room next door would have plenty to say.

She looked starved to death, but the bits of food she had eaten in the past three days had begun to add some color to her pretty face. She would come around.

Would Frank and Michelle be ready for the answers that she gave?

Three Days Later

Josie stumbled out of the bed room in a pair of Michelle's sweats and a too big t-shirt of Franks'. She eyed Michelle sheepishly waiting for her to say something... anything.

When she continued to just stare Josie muttered that she was sure she would have some explaining to do. But first she asked Michelle – was she a cop?

Michelle shook her head and slowly smiled. What would the child think? "How about we get you something to eat and decent clothes? We can wait for Frank if you want but I am starving."

Josie smiled back. "Thank you for letting me sleep."

After meeting with Frank at the pizza place down the road for a vegetarian supreme and two large root beers the three some went back to the room.

Josie told them everything. How they had come to the meeting in the woods. The deaths of Steven, Wes and Thomas. How she had wound up in the White Bayou in Texas. How and why she had shot her brothers and sisters.

Michelle and Frank listened.

Josie told them of the deaths of Nancy and Carrie. She even went back to tell them of her brother Patrick's going to God.

After she had finished they all sat in silence for awhile before Josie got up and headed for her room.

Michelle jumped to her feet and reached for what was left of the young girl with tears streaming down both of their faces. "You can stay with us. We will never repeat what you have had to see... to do. You can be happy and safe with us. We promise."

Michelle looked to where Frank nodded his agreement.

Josie just smiled and wiped at her tears. "Right now I just want to sleep."

Josie lay awake for a couple of hours before sneaking out of their room.

She went to look around... down alleys, through windows, into taverns. So this is what they had been missing. Nothing at all...

The violence raged on. There were drunks in the

alleys passed out. There were ladies of the night hanging on street corners. There were children lying alone staring at a TV. There were a couple doing drugs in one of the bottom apartments where she walked by. She knew the smell.

No. They had it way better in the parks. That was were her family lie.

Josie went back to the hotel to her bed room and dug out the .22.

Chapter Forty-Two

Michelle and Frank dealt with the questioning for another hour before tracking down Maranda and turning Josies file over to her.

They had enough drama for the night.

They kept a lot of Josie's story to themselves for the moment.

There were plenty of other children. Some of them could be saved. There were plenty of good people to do the saving.

When they had checked into another hotel for the night and fallen straight into bed they curled up in each others arms.

"She was worth it." Michelle smiled a tiny smile.

"Yes she was." Frank replied simply before kissing her good night. "It was good to meet her, to know her as well as we could. It will help in understanding the others. It gives us the means to talk to them."

Michelle flipped back over to stare at Frank.

"So we are not giving up?"

Frank hugged his best friend close. "Never."

Chapter Forty-Three

Josie awoke in a pool of bright light. Emily was sitting near a camp fire on the left side of a beautiful man... with Thomas and Wes, Shelley, Kevin, Lil' Dawne, Darryl, John and Tracy, Nancy, Joy and Carrie...

"You see Josie. We did it right. We came home..." Emily walked over and extended her arms to Josie. "Thanks Josie. Thank You for sending us home."

God Forgives.

Fran Hinton was born and raised in the Midwest but is currently residing in the South. When not busy banging away on the keys she likes to plant things... See how they grow. God Bless.